home for the holidays

Boston Grizzlies Hockey Club

Book 1.5

allie lasky

boston grizzlies hockey club

Reading Order

Here is the recommended reading order for this series:

Tending Her Heart (Seb and Audrey)

Puck Me Twice (Sven and Vanessa)

Home for the Holidays (Jake and Rachel)

Body Check (Jason and Amelia)

Defenseless (Ryan and Hailey)

Power Play (Al and Riley)

Game Misconduct (Nick and Bex)

Instigator (Aidan and Ceci)

One Timer (Adam and Avery)

Delay of Game (Parker and Ivy)

one

. . .

Rachel

MY STUPID FUCKING boyfriend is a stupid fuckface.

Then again, that's not really *news*. He's always been a stupid fuckface. I just didn't see it.

Six and a half years. That's how long I wasted on that asshole.

It wasn't all bad. There were good moments in there. That's how he was able to keep me shackled to him for that long Hell, he finally asked me to move in with him late last year, convincing me he was actually ready to commit. He kept stringing me along, promising things like marriage and babies, taunting me with a future he had no intention of ever following through on. So: I'm thirty-one, I'm single, and I'm suddenly homeless, because I can't stand the sight of his stupid fucking face for one goddamn minute more.

Oh, and it's the holidays.

All of my friends are coupled up. I could crash with them for a day or two, but the constant sex noises when I am decidedly *not* getting any really don't help with my piss-poor mood.

"I've got a solution," Mom tells me over our weekly Zoom call.

I'm crashing at my friends Arielle and Asher's place, and they've gone out for the evening on a date. I'll have to sleep with my noise-canceling headphones on. They weren't quiet back when Arielle and I lived together in our old apartment; I can't ask them to keep it down when I'm a guest in their house.

I roll my eyes. "I'm not moving home, Ma."

"Psh." She waves a hand at me. "I wasn't going to suggest it."

Except she has—repeatedly. Technically, I could work a hybrid schedule, teaching a few days a week, being in the lab as much as possible, and spending the rest of the time in New Hampshire with her, but commute aside, the idea is less than ideal.

"The Lewis boy," she says.

I frown. "Josh? My high school boyfriend?"

We haven't talked to each other in years. Sometimes I go home for the High Holy Days, and we might chat a bit in the lobby of the temple, but it's been at least five years since I've seen him.

"No, the other one. The cute one, with the curly hair." She sighs and shakes her head. "Anyway, I was talking to Becky Lewis at temple the other day, and she mentioned her boy lives in Boston now."

Squinting, I try to remember which of Josh's brothers she's talking about. One is a hockey player, at least last I heard, and the other is… kind of a nerd.

Jeremy was on the debate team and did Model U.N. We were in the robotics club together my senior year. I think he was a sophomore that year, so we didn't interact much more than Josh and I driving him home from school things. From what I can remember, he was fine.

Well. I like nerds. I can handle nerds. It totally won't be awkward that I dated his older brother fifteen years ago. Hell, I haven't even talked to Josh since college. There were a couple of times we ran into each other at home over summer break, and we were always amicable, but we were never going to have that epic love story I dreamed about.

We were in high school. We dated. We went to college. We broke up.

That's it. That's the whole story.

"*Anyway*," Ma says, "the Lewis boy has an extra room in his apartment. Becky says he's never home, always traveling for work. You'd practically have the place for yourself."

"How much is the rent?" I have a bit saved up, but the rental market is slim picking this time of year. It may take a while before I'm able to find a place on my own—even if that's with roommates.

"Don't worry about that," Ma says.

I roll my eyes. "I kind of have to make sure I can afford it."

"Well, Becky didn't tell me an amount," she snaps. "Do you want the boy's number or not?"

"Yes, please," I mumble.

———

There's a spring in my step as I head into the lab. I haven't felt this buoyant in the weeks since Erik dumped me over dinner.

We were sitting on the couch, eating Thai food, when he announced that he was bored and wanted to try something new. I thought he meant a new Thai place. Or maybe even a new sex position, because let's face it, that was getting a little old.

No. He meant *new*. He didn't want me anymore. He was done.

But I won't let that fuckface ruin this gorgeous day.

The sun is shining, it's a beautiful fall day with the faintest crisp to the air, and I have our monthly staff meeting today—which means I get *donuts*.

I love donuts, don't get me wrong, but I don't let myself

eat them outside of staff meetings or other occasions when they are provided for me. After an unfortunate few months in grad school that led me to gaining thirty pounds and spending *way* too much money at Dunkin', I had to cut myself off. It was a necessary fact of life, even if I'm still not happy about it.

Erik refused to buy me donuts. He didn't want me to *lose my figure.*

What he didn't understand is that it's my body and I'm the one living in it. If I want to be a size six or a size sixteen or even a size twenty-six, that's up to me; he doesn't get to enforce his "body standards" on me.

"You look happy," Hattie says when I swing into the conference room.

"I am." I look over the selection of pastries on the table. There's no donuts, just croissants, cookies, and muffins. "I *was.* Where are the donuts?"

"Jan wanted to try a new bakery." Hattie winces. "I'm *sorry.*"

"It's not your fault, you didn't do anything."

"I know. I'm still sorry."

"You're so Canadian." I shake my head with a smile.

No matter how many times we've stared in the mirror together and repeated our mantra—I am a badass bitch — she still feels the need to apologize for everything. It's the Ottawa upbringing, she says.

"We'll go out for lunch," she offers. "I'll buy you a donut."

"Thanks, babe."

As the rest of the staff files in for the meeting, we dig into the pastries—still delicious, even if they aren't donuts—and discuss the projects on our plate. The industry is winding down for the year. We get three full weeks off at the end of the year, plus there's the holiday party and a few things with our clients.

It'll be nice to have some time to relax and recalibrate. Maybe find a new apartment. Maybe I'll even get a cat.

All I have to do is call the Lewis kid.

two

. . .

Jake

HOLY FUCK.

I have a text from Rachel Levine.

That's a name I haven't heard in… a decade? Maybe more.

I hurry to sit upright and slap myself in the face with my phone.

"You okay there, bud?" my teammate and friend, Sven Larsson, asks from the second bed of our shared hotel room.

Normally, veterans don't have to share hotel rooms, but since he started dating our team's Logistics coordinator, Coach has been putting him in a room with someone else to *discourage fraternization*. Despite the fact their relationship is officially declared with HR and management.

Me, I'm that weirdo that volunteered for it. I don't like to stay in hotel rooms by myself. It gets too lonely, and then I get self-destructive, and frankly, it's better for all of us if I'm not left to my own devices.

"Fuck off," I mutter in our own twisted love language, and he smirks at me.

I turn my attention back to my phone.

Rachel Levine.

Fuck.

I can't even be upset at my mother giving out my phone number *again*. This time, it doesn't seem like she's matchmaking, merely offering up my spare room now that Jeremy moved out.

Although…

Rachel was the source of my sexual awakening. It was a little awkward at the time, considering she was dating my older brother Josh, but hey, I was always stealing his toys as the shit-stirring youngest brother—is it really too much of a stretch for me to want his girl, too?

Also, he treated her like shit. Always ignoring her, canceling plans last minute to hang with his other friends, generally being a teenage dirtbag.

I was too young to do anything about it back then.

> Hi, yes, my roommate moved out and I have an empty room.

Calling Jeremy my roommate is a little less pathetic than saying "my big brother" in this context.

> I'm out of town but get back on Thursday. Do you want to come see the place?

> What's the rent?

Hm.

"Hey, asshole," I say out loud, and Sven looks up. I snicker because he actually answered to that. "What's the going price for rent these days?"

"Fuck if I know," he shrugs. "Want me to ask Van?"

"Would you?"

His girlfriend, Vanessa, works for the team in the Logistics department. She's fucking awesome. She travels about half-time with the team, and this road trip is one she's back in the office for. Something about planning the team's annual holiday season activities.

A few minutes later, Sven names a number, and I text it back to Rachel.

> Are you fucking with me?

No?

> Every apartment I've seen is, like, twice that.

It's a really shitty apartment.

> I'll take it.

You haven't even seen the room yet.

> For that price? I can't not take it.

That doesn't make me feel good. That makes me feel decidedly *not* good.

> I'm desperate. Even if it's just for a month or two, I really appreciate it.

You got it!

I text her the address.

Meet me Thursday anytime after 2.

That'll give me enough time to clean up after morning skate.

There's a giddiness in my heart when she confirms the date and time. An itchy restlessness in my bones. I can't sit here in my hotel room bed and pretend like this isn't the best fucking thing to happen to me in weeks—no, *months*.

Sven looks over at me suspiciously. "What's wrong with your face?"

"Nothing. What's wrong with *your* face?" I counter.

He frowns. "You look weird."

"I need to get out of here." I don't know where I'm going to go, just that I can't stay here.

Swiping my hotel key card off the nightstand, I slide on my sandals and go walking through the hallways. I'm not about to *leave* the property—management would have my head—and I don't want to head to the bar. It's no surprise when I end up in the rinky-dink little gym. There are two treadmills, two recumbent bikes, and a weight bench that's seen better days.

I'm not properly warmed up, plus I'm scheduled to start in the game tomorrow evening, so I keep to a brisk pace as I walk and walk and walk.

Rachel Levine.

Do I want a roommate? Not really. When Jeremy needed a place to stay for a few months between jobs, I didn't mind when he moved in. I'd just signed my big contract extension and was feeling the post-signing letdown. The crush of everyone's expectations could have gotten me into a bad place.

Luckily, my brother was there to help pump me up on the bad nights, and now two years later, I'm a bona fide starting goaltender rather than part of an A/B tendy tandem. Henry, my backup goaltender, is a good guy, but he's still green.

Jer stayed for longer than either of us expected. It was kind of nice having my brother around. Josh would have been a massive dick to live with, mainly because he's a massive dick in all other aspects of his life. He's still pissed our parents decided to have two more children after he was born. It's like, dude, get over it. Jeremy is twenty-nine and I'm twenty-six. It's not like they're suddenly going to change their minds about having us as part of the family.

I wonder if this will make things more awkward with us, then immediately dismiss the thought. It's not like I talk to my brother all that much to begin with. He dated Rachel for a hot minute in high school. He's a grown ass adult now. If he's still pining after his high school girlfriend more than fifteen years later, he has bigger problems than my lending her a spare room.

And if she's my roommate, I can't ask her out. Not that I know anything about her as an adult. She could be a heinous bitch who talks down to everyone.

No. The Rachel Levine I knew back then was kind and sweet—not to mention hot as fuck. I consider looking up her social media, but that feels like an invasion of privacy. I don't post much on my "official" account, mainly using it to message with the boys and send memes to Jer.

Some guys use social media to hook up, but one, it's hard to gauge chemistry online, and two, I don't necessarily want a trail of evidence of all the women in my past. Most of the women I take home, I meet at the bar after a game. It might be boring and predictable, but it works for a reason.

And let me just say, there's nothing to draw some attention like a crowd of hyped-up, post-game hockey players in suits. Thank goodness the league forces us to wear the suits pre- and post-game.

I wonder if Rachel would ever come to a game. Maybe I could even convince her to come to the bar after, too. And then we'd go home together, to the apartment that we'll be sharing...

I shiver in anticipation. Yes. This. I like this.

I can't sleep with her, I wouldn't ever do anything to make her uncomfortable while she's staying in my house, but even if it only lasts for a little while, it will be nice to have someone to go home with.

Someone to come home to.

three

. . .

Rachel

THE GUY who answers the door is *not* Jeremy Lewis. In an instant, I realize I've made a terrible mistake.

"Hey, Rachel," the big, strong, broad guy says in a surprisingly deep voice.

"Jake. Hi. I didn't recognize you."

Last I saw him, Jake Lewis was fifteen years old, pimply and wearing braces, a lanky string bean in oversized hockey sweaters.

This guy…

Jake Lewis is hot.

He's tall, well over six foot, and nearly as wide across the chest. He's wearing a white button-down shirt with the sleeves rolled up his strong forearms. The fabric stretches taut across his biceps, like the seams can barely contain his muscles. His nose looks like it's been broken more than once, and his short beard adds definition to his strong jawline. He smells like Irish Spring soap and that little humanizing fact makes me lose my nerve.

I can't do this.

"I didn't realize you lived in Boston," I say casually as I follow him into the apartment. It's on the twentieth floor of a ritzy, fifty-floor building. There's no way I'll be able to afford the rent here. Even splitting the rent with another person—or five—it has *got* to be way out of my budget.

"Moved out here a few years ago. They decided to keep me," Jake says, running a hand over his short hair.

"They?"

"The Grizzlies," he coughs.

I blink. "You're still playing hockey?"

Guarded, he nods.

"You're playing hockey for the *Grizzlies*?" My voice goes up in pitch.

Jake chews the inside of his lip as he nods again.

"Fuck, that's awesome!" I reach for him, then pause. "That's really fantastic, Jake. I know how much hockey always meant to you."

He clears his throat. "You didn't know? I thought my mother told everyone back at temple."

"My mom probably told me in the middle of an epic kvetching session," I try to play it off. "I'm not really involved in the gossip train."

His weak smile tells me I'm not successful.

"What do you need a roommate for? If you're playing for the Grizzlies, you can probably afford to live alone."

Shit. I probably wasn't supposed to say that.

"I prefer to have someone else in the apartment, especially with how often I travel," Jake says casually.

"Oh. Right." I forgot about that. He's probably on the road all the time. Good. That means I won't have to see too much of him.

"Besides, you need a place to stay," he continues. "It's not like I could tell you to kick rocks when I have a perfectly functional spare room."

"I mean, you could."

Jake shrugs. "Yeah, but I won't."

"Why aren't you?" I turn it back to him.

"Because I won't," he says, like it's that simple.

And maybe, for him, it is.

He clears his throat again. "Let me show you the place."

The living room is understated, simple black and white with a dark blue accent wall. His furniture is similarly simple, too, a leather sectional and armchair center by a glass coffee table. Through the open living room, I can see a stark, clean, black and white kitchen with stools at the marble countertop.

"This is the living area," Jake says, waving at the space. A giant TV is mounted on the blue accent wall. "I have all the streaming channels plus cable, whatever you need."

My eyebrows go up. "You have cable?" I didn't think anyone under the age of 40 had cable anymore.

He shrugs. "I like it. Plus with all the blackouts, I can't watch half the college football games if I don't have cable."

"You're still a Michigan fan?" I tease.

He was too young to do the recruitment thing when I knew him, but even back then, his eyes had been on the Maize and Blue and the NHL, knowing college hockey would get him to the big leagues.

And it did. Clearly, it paid off for him.

"Yeah. Go Blue," Jake says without a hint of sarcasm. "Took my squad to the Frozen Four two years running."

I notice he didn't say he *won* the Frozen Four. That's probably something I shouldn't ask about, either.

"And now you're with the Grizzlies."

"They drafted me. I spent some time with the minor league team before they called me up. Signed an extension three years ago. I'm here to stay now."

I shake my head. "Must be nice."

"Yeah. It is," he says, with a hint of steel in his voice. "Why are you here, Rachel?"

"I need a place to stay." I swallow nervously. "If you don't want me here—"

"How did a girl like you wind up needing to move in with a virtual stranger?"

I scrub a hand over my face. "Because I'm dumb."

"Don't say that." He pulls my arm away from my face. "You're not dumb. You're a fucking nuclear physicist."

Forcing a laugh, I taunt back, "So I guess I'm not the only one in the gossip circles."

Jake shakes his head. "Nah. I looked you up."

My eyes go wide.

"Had to make sure I wasn't offering my place up to a serial killer."

"I promise I'm not a serial killer," I tell him dryly. "I just… my boyfriend and I broke up, and I couldn't stand the idea of staying in our apartment for a freaking day more, so I moved out with no plan. And then I realized I'm thirty-one and can't crash on my friends' couches anymore. So… here I am."

He squeezes my elbow. "Well, I'm glad you're here."

My stomach leaps. "You are?"

"Yeah. It'll be great to catch up. Like summer camp," Jake says with a broad grin.

I snort out a laugh.

"Come on. Let me show you to your room."

The bedroom is basic, already situated with a bed, nightstand, and a small desk and chair. Across the hallway is a bathroom with a sleek, shiny, silver shower.

"My office is through here," he says, pointing at another door.

"You have an office?"

He laughs. "I don't use it much. If you need to work from home or whatever, you can use it."

"Most of my work has to be done in the lab or in the lecture hall," I say carefully.

"Yeah. Right. That makes sense." He nods a few times. "Well, the offer is there."

I lift my chin toward the last door. "That's your room?"

His cheeks flush pink. "Yeah. Do you, uh, want to see it?"

My eyebrows go up. "Uh… sure?"

He leads me down the short hallway to his bedroom. And then my jaw drops.

The first thing that strikes me is the view. He has floor-to-ceiling windows overlooking downtown below. The room is huge—funnily enough, that is not the first thing to register. An enormous bed is situated in the middle, with a recliner by the windows. His bed is haphazardly made, like he just tossed the blankets back over the mattress in a rush.

That makes me think about what he'd look like in that bed, his strong body warm and cuddly, his hair rumpled from sleep.

No. It's entirely inappropriate to lust over my new roommate. It's even more inappropriate to think about what he'd look like underneath that white button-down straining over his strong muscles.

Jake clears his throat. "You okay?"

Startled, I nod, turning to check out his bathroom. "Yeah. I'm—holy *fuck*."

He has a soaker tub. A giant, claw-foot, old-fashioned soaker tub.

"I—you—will you marry me?" I blurt.

He chokes. "What?"

"That's inappropriate." I squeeze my eyes shut and try to recalibrate. "Your tub. That's gorgeous."

His eyes widen. "Well, you can use it anytime."

"Oh. No. I couldn't—I wouldn't want to impose."

"Rachel." Jake reaches out and squeezes my arm again. "You are many things, but you are not an imposition."

And when he says it… I almost believe him.

four

. . .

Jake

"I HAVE A PROBLEM," I announce to the room of half-naked men.

Instantly, the locker room falls silent. We're getting ready for pre-game skate, preparing for tonight's game against Minnesota.

"What do you need, bro?" MacGregor asks. An assistant captain, he's always there to lend a hand.

"I need…" I scrub my hand over my face. "I need to get laid."

"We'll go out to the bar after the game," Gonzo says. "We'll be your wingmen."

"I can't."

Gonzo raises his eyebrows. "Is it, like, a performance issue? I've heard rumors…"

"Fuck you, no, you haven't," I snap back. "It's not something to be ashamed of, if there *were* issues. But that's not my problem."

"So what's going on?" MacGregor pushes.

"I offered up my spare room to an old family friend."

"So now you can't bring a chick back to your place to get it on?" Logan asks.

"*She's* the one I want to get it on with." I sink onto the bench in front of my locker stall. "She's entirely off limits. But, fuck…"

"Is she hot?" Pope asks. He's a dick of epic proportions on a good day.

I glare at him. "You're not touching her."

He raises his hands in mock innocence. "I wasn't going to."

With a sigh, I admit, "She's fucking gorgeous. And now she's staying at my place until she gets back on her feet."

"Or you get her on her back," Pope snarks.

Flipping him off, I look to the rest of the guys in the room. "What do I do?"

"Well, don't bring another girl back to your place. That's asking for trouble," McKittrick says. As the oldest on the team, he's usually thought to be the dad of the group. Although, considering he's fresh off a divorce, maybe he isn't the best to ask for advice…

"Is there a reason you can't ask her out?" Larsson asks. "If she says no—"

"If she says no, she'll feel awkward in my apartment, and that's the last thing I want." I rub my eye. "I want it to be a safe place for her. I'm not in a hurry for her to leave."

"How long has she been there?" MacGregor asks.

"She's moving in today."

He snorts. "Well, bro, you're fucked."

"Not the way I'd like to be."

"Send her tickets to the game," McKittrick says. "Invite her to the bar after. If she's going to be your new roommate, let her all the way into your life."

"I don't want to scare her away, either, though."

He shrugs. "Well, if you want a chance with her, you've got to show her what your life is really like. Don't sugarcoat things. Be real, or don't bother."

With a hum, I turn over what he's saying. It doesn't make

sense to pretend to be anyone else. Rachel is either going to like me or she won't. But I don't have a chance at anything with her if I don't show her my real, true self.

"Thanks, dude," I finally say, and McKittrick gives me a smug smile. "Not too shabby for an old guy."

His smile falls. "Fuck off, asshole."

With a laugh, I turn back to my locker stall and continue getting prepped for tonight. We still have a good deal of time before we have to be out there for pre-game skate.

Fishing my phone out of my bag, I pull up my text thread with Rachel. She hasn't responded since she confirmed the access code worked earlier this morning.

Before I can overthink it, I send her two tickets to the players' friends and family suite, then email Vanessa in the Logistics department to get her on the VIP list.

> Here's two tickets to tonight's game. We're all going out to the Pigeon after the game. No pressure if you're not interested.

The little text bubble jumps as she types, then goes away. She types some more, then stops.

"Dude, relax," Henry says. He's the other half of our goaltending team. "You're going to get worked up again."

And we all know what that means, he doesn't say.

Instead of shutting out all goals, I let every goal pass through me like a sieve, and then he gets called in to mind the net when it's supposed to be his night off.

Goaltending is a mentally strenuous job. It's a physical game, but the mental fortitude it takes to stay still while vulcanized rubber discs are aimed directly at your soft tissue at a hundred miles an hour—and to do it on purpose…

But I didn't choose to be a goaltender, the goaltending life chose me. It makes me happy.

If I couldn't be a goaltender, I'd be *fine* playing on a line with other guys. I could score goals. I could bulldoze anyone who tries to cross the blue line. But it wouldn't be the same as standing guard over the net, the last remaining line of defense between my team and a loss.

Does it feel *good* when I let a shot past me? No, not really. I've had my fair share of losing games. After all, I've been playing hockey since I was four and in the net full-time since I was seven. The coaches used to try to get us to switch positions every few games, but from the get-go, I knew I wanted to tend goal, and they finally let me stay where I wanted.

It's my happy place.

When the time comes for us to head out for warmups, I take the ice with all of my usual bravado. It's time to focus. It's time to get to work.

Still, my eyes rise to the rafters, wondering if she's up there, wondering if she can see me. Does Rachel even like hockey?

Scratch that—how can anyone *not* like hockey?

I let my body lead me through the warmup relying on muscle memory. After doing this for so many years, I have a routine, part superstition, part habit. I stretch and twist and get my blades familiar with the ice, digging the toe of my skate in to create little divots. My posts are there to protect me, and I make sure they get a good dousing from my water bottle. My stick taps the edge of the blue paint, marking my territory.

And when we head back into the locker room for our final pre-game pep talk, I don't check my phone. It's barely even on my radar.

That's a lie. It's definitely on my mind, weighing me down. Will she be there?

But I don't allow myself to check. I have a job to do.

It's game time.

five

. . .

Rachel

I SHOULDN'T BE HERE.

When Jake sent me the tickets, I almost said no. How can he expect me to get to the arena on no notice? I need, like, a solid three to four *days* to prep for being social.

But when faced with the idea of staying alone in his apartment all evening…

So I pulled on my big-girl pants and left the apartment, meeting up with my friend Viv. She's a rugby player on Boston's pro team and has gone to the Olympics twice with the national team. She is also bitterly sarcastic and totally outgoing, which is what I need right about now.

"So tell me about the guy," Viv says as we walk to our seats. We've been to games with our friend Ceci before, we've shared a box with other people, but we've never been to a *suite.*

"He's my ex's kid brother," I explain.

She rolls her eyes. "Okay, I mean, is he hot, is he single…?"

"Oh. I don't know."

"You don't know if he's hot?"

My face heats. "He's a child."

Viv stops in her tracks. "What?"

"He's, like, twenty-six."

"That's not a child. So you definitely wouldn't be robbing the cradle," she decides, already determining that I'm into him.

Which I am. Or maybe I'm not. I don't know.

"He's a baby," I insist, although I don't really know why I'm pushing the point. The five years between us are almost a lifetime. He may be a professional hockey player, but he's probably still an immature, overgrown frat boy athlete living the high life. There's no way—it's totally inappropriate.

And there's that word again. Why am I so worried about what is appropriate and what's not? Since when do I care about the optics of everything?

"You don't have to marry the guy. He can still be a fun rebound," Viv suggests. She sighs. "After the douchebag…"

"I've been calling him fuckface," I admit.

"Fine. After what fuckface did, you deserve a little lighthearted fun," she says. "You're living with a professional hockey player now. He sent you a ticket to the game. He obviously wants you here."

"He's just being nice."

She rolls her eyes. "Nice would have been nosebleed seats. He didn't have to invite you out after the game. He could have just said, *see you at home, roomie.*"

That doesn't sit right with me.

"He's only doing this because our moms are friends."

Viv shrugs. "Whatever his reasoning, he's doing it. Might as well make the most of the opportunity."

Humming, I follow her into the suite. There are close to a dozen other women in here, each one glammed up and looking fierce in bedazzled Boston Grizzlies jerseys. Heads swivel toward us as we enter.

A blonde woman with a baby bump approaches us. "Hi,

I'm Melanie Easton. My husband is Mark, the second line center. Who are you here with?"

"I'm a friend of Jake's. Lewis," I struggle to get the words out. "He invited us."

Two women in the back of the suite exchange looks.

"We love Jake," another blonde says, coming over to join us. "I'm Hailey MacGregor. My brother Aidan says he's a great guy."

"Oh, we're not—I'm not—"

"If you say so." Hailey smiles gently. "Typically, it's just family up here. Jake must really care for you."

I'm introduced to the other women. Three are wives, two are fiancées, one more is a sister, and there's a mom, too. There are no girlfriends. Huh. I wonder what it means that Jake invited me up here.

Hailey looks to be about Jake's age. She leads us to the back of the suite, where there's a buffet set up and a bucket of chilled drinks. I hand a bottle of water to Viv, who doesn't drink, and grab a hard seltzer for myself.

When Jake said he played for the Grizzlies, my dumb ass thought he was, like, a back-up third-string forward, someone who gets called up when they need a warm body. Even a warm body in the NHL is an amazing achievement.

But when I see number 1 Lewis take up a stance in front of the goal…

"I think I'm in trouble," I tell Viv.

"What's wrong?"

Nodding to Jake, I explain, "He's a goaltender."

"And?"

"And that's fucking hot," I whisper. "He's the caretaker of the team. He carries them on his back every night."

I bet he'd *take care of* me all night long. Repeatedly.

"And that's a bad thing because…"

"Because I can't sleep with him."

Her eyebrows go up. "But you want to?"

Rolling my eyes, I pull out my phone and flip to his Instagram page. "Look at him."

The first photo, he's wearing his jersey and a blue and white Santa hat, pushing a giant shopping cart filled with toys.

The second photo?

Jake is shirtless, his bulging arms crossed over his broad chest, and the cheesiest grin on his face.

"Okay, yeah, I can see what you mean," Viv says. "I didn't think you were interested in meatheads."

"He's not a meathead," I defend.

Viv waves the phone. "By definition, a meathead. Trust me, I'd know."

She's the oldest of six siblings, five of whom are professional athletes. Including her.

"He's completely different than Erik. Physically, that is." She squints at the phone. "Is his chest waxed?"

"I'm sure it's just shaved," I mutter.

"He's definitely wearing body oil," she continues. "He's gorgeous. Fuck, if you don't go after him, I will."

"I'm not *going after* him. He's giving me a place to stay."

"Yeah, and you can give his cock a place to stay." She waggles her eyebrows.

"Gross."

"Seriously, Rach." Viv sets her hand on my arm. "You deserve a little casual fun with a nice guy. It doesn't have to be with this dude. It doesn't have to be forever. It can just be a little bit of fun for now."

"I dated his brother," I remind her.

"Yeah. When you were in high school. That doesn't count," she retorts.

Glancing around us, I lower my voice. "I slept with his brother."

"Was it good?"

I shrug. "I mean, it was both of our first time. It... he

wasn't *great.*" We were having sex as often as possible for two teenagers who lived at home for maybe six months before we ended things. It didn't get much better. It wasn't until college that I realized what sex was supposed to be like.

I guess it was too much to expect Josh to suddenly be devoted and doting in bed. Then again, he was kind of a dick out of bed, too.

"Then let the kid brother show up the older brother." Viv smirks.

I wince. "And let him brag about me to Josh? Gross."

She shrugs. "So don't go for it. Let someone else snap him up."

"He's not a cookie at a dessert bar."

"No," Viv agrees. "He's the entire buffet, ready for your taking."

six

· · ·

Jake

WE WIN. It's a glorious win, too, four goals to one.

I'm flying high as we shuttle down the chute toward the locker room. Flinging myself onto the locker stall bench, I sit there for a moment and breathe, taking it all in.

My phone buzzes in my locker, and swiveling in my seat, I reach for it. There's a bunch of messages on the screen, but my eyes narrow in on the most recent.

Good game. Where should I meet you?

I gave her the address of the bar already.

"Hey," I nudge MacGregor. "Where does Hailey usually meet you?"

"In the tunnel?" He cocks his head. "Wait, did you send your girl to the WAGs suite?"

Slowly, I nod. "Should I not?"

He shakes his head. "I'll handle it."

Reaching for his phone, he taps on the screen, and when it buzzes in response, he looks up at me. "Hailey's got her and her friend. She'll bring them to us."

"Thanks, dude." I give him a fist-bump.

"For future reference," MacGregor lowers his voice. "The box is for the people who are committed to being by our sides. Wives, fiancées, family. Girlfriends sit at ice level."

I feel my face heat, and because I'm not wearing my pads, I'm able to feel it spread down my chest. Hopefully, the guys chalk it up to a post-game flush.

"She's not my girlfriend," I mutter. *I just want her to be.*

He shakes his head. "Be careful, man. I hope you know what you're getting yourself into."

After a few minutes, I peel out of my pads and pants to my base layer and head to the bikes to recover. How am I going to play this? What am I going to say?

I think about it all through the cooldown and during my shower. I'm still thinking about it when I pull on my post-game suit and style my hair with a little more care than usual.

MacGregor catches my eye, hiding a smirk. "You ready?"

Tying off my dress shoe, I blow out a breath and shake out my hands. "Yeah. Let's do this."

Followed by Larsson, Easton, and Logan, we head to the players' tunnels connecting the locker rooms to the parking structure. Logan is the only other one of us unattached, but he's been down lately, so I don't mind him tagging along.

"Hey, boo," Melanie, Easton's wife, says as we approach. "Good game." She's followed by Hailey MacGregor, Rachel, and her friend.

Easton is such a fucking sap, because he melts when she wraps her arms around him. "You're my good luck charm."

I force a laugh. "I think you mean me. *I'm* your good luck charm."

He punches me in the shoulder. "Fuck off."

"Hey." I nod to Rachel. "How are you?"

"Good. You played—wow, you played really well," she says, wringing her hands. "Thanks for the tickets."

Her friend, a tall, muscular woman with her hair in a ponytail, nods. "Thanks for including me."

"I'm Jake," I introduce, offering my hand.

"Viv Gallagher. I play with the Revolution. It was cool to see how you guys do things," she says.

"No shit. You play rugby?" My eyebrows go up.

She nods. "Yeah. Our season is over for the year."

MacGregor nods. "Rugby is totally cool."

As all of the attention swivels to Viv, my focus is on Rachel. She seems to shrink into herself, a smile on her face like she's content to let her friend take the spotlight.

I clear my throat. "Did you want to grab a drink before we head home?"

Rachel and Viv share a loaded look.

"I'm not sure…" Rachel starts, then stops.

"I can be around it without needing to partake," Viv says. She looks to me. "I'm sober."

"Logan can give you a ride home," MacGregor offers, clapping our single teammate on the shoulder.

The man in question winces. "Yeah, totally."

Oh, good, so I'm not the only one who's noticed him staring wistfully at MacGregor's sister. *That* is a recipe for disaster.

"I can hang out for a little bit," Viv says, shaking her head. "Thanks, though."

Easton laughs. "You guys have fun. We're headed out."

"See you," MacGregor says, lifting a hand to wave. "Hailes, you ready?" He wraps his arm around his little sister's shoulder.

She nods, looking between us and Logan, then to Rachel and Viv. "You'll take care of them?"

I meet her eyes. "We're good."

Satisfied, she lets her brother lead her over to their car. I hook my thumb over my shoulder. "I parked that way."

"See you there," Logan announces, a defeated expression on his face. He tucks his hands into his pockets and walks toward his car.

I want to fix this. I want to make it better for him. But even I know that trying to ask out his teammate's little sister is a bad idea.

My car is a "basic" black SUV—a luxury SUV, that is. Some guys go for the Porsche or Maserati. I'm more than happy with a plain, black Mercedes with all the tech bells and whistles. I'm not a car guy, I just need to get from Point A to Point B. Josh is the one into cars and motors.

I think that's why I've always stayed away from it. Not because I didn't want to take it away from him—I'd *love* to take away his toys. More because he's such a territorial asshole, it wasn't worth the fight.

And cars are boring to me, to top it off. If I were actually interested, it would be different. Where it counts, I hold my ground.

Rachel slides into the front seat beside me. Her sweet perfume fills the car cabin, settling that itch inside my soul that never really seems to go away. She's so close—I could just reach across and grab her hand, or set my hand on her knee.

But that would be weird. So I don't.

Even though I want to.

After we get out of the parking structure, we're dumped straight into traffic. You'd think an hour after the game, it would have dissipated some. Instead, it seems to have gotten worse.

Once we're out of the thick of it, it's a quick ten minute drive to the bar. It's loud and raucous, and the bouncer lets the three of us in without a second glance. Setting my hand on the smalls of their backs, I lead Rachel and Viv up to the VIP section where we hang out.

"You made it!" Vanessa exclaims when she catches sight of us. She's wrapped around Larsson, who looks blissfully happy. He was a sad sack when they were fighting earlier this year. I'm glad they've patched things up.

To my surprise, Rachel and Viv both give her hugs.

"You… know each other?" I ask cautiously.

"We're in the same book club," Rachel explains.

"Imagine my surprise when you added them to the VIP list," Vanessa teases.

"Another friend, Sadie, her boyfriend works for the team, too," Viv adds. "And then Ceci… Well, let's just say, we're big fans of the team."

"And yet you didn't know I played for the team," I grin at Rachel.

She flushes. "I didn't realize it was you. It's a common name."

"There is another Lewis in the league, he plays for Edmonton," I tell her. "I get it. You're, like, totally obsessed with me."

Rachel snorts out a laugh. "Yeah, okay. Glad to see your ego is still enormous."

"Among other things." I waggle my eyebrows at her, and she giggles.

"I need a drink," she announces. "How do we get drinks?"

"I've got it. What do you want?" Vanessa says.

"Just a water," Rachel says. She turns to Viv. "Same?"

The rugby player nods. "Thanks."

"I didn't realize you and Van knew each other," I say casually. "Imagine, we could have been hanging out all this time."

"Yeah." Rachel's voice is weak. Her eyes dart around the club. "We should sit. Can we sit?"

"I'm going to catch up with Robby," Viv says, nodding toward our team's equipment manager.

"You know Andrews?" He used to be a goalie before he blew out his knee, so he's always kept a bit of distance from me. I can't imagine sitting on the sidelines and watching someone else do the things I love most.

"He's friends with my brother," she says simply. "They played in juniors together."

I blink. "Who's your brother?"

She sighs. "Chuck Gallagher."

"He's with… Colorado?"

Viv nods.

"So you're, like, really connected." My mind is blown. "How have we not met before? I mean, you play for Boston, and your family is in the league, and…"

Viv's eyes dart to Rachel. "I don't know."

Right. Rachel. The whole reason I'm here.

"Let's sit," I remember her request, guiding her over to a loveseat sofa and armchair. To my surprise, when I sit down on the couch, she sits right beside me. "You okay?"

"A little overwhelmed," Rachel admits. "I didn't expect you and Viv to hit it off so well. I should have, though. You're both athletes."

Is it just my imagination, or does she sound bitter?

"Professional networking," I tell her honestly. "It would be the same if you went to a conference for physicists, right?"

She shrugs. "It's just… a lot."

"Moving is a lot. I can't imagine doing all of that today on top of all of this." Waving my hand at the crowded bar, I take it all in. "If you're not used to this…"

"I'm just wound up. I'll relax," Rachel says firmly.

"Okay. If you need any help with that, let me know."

Her eyebrow arches up. "How would you help me relax?"

"I don't know. Shoulder rub? You could soak in my tub?" I purposefully don't mention my favorite form of naked stress relief. That would be *inappropriate*, as she said earlier. This little crush I have on her is going to be extremely inconvenient.

There needs to be boundaries. Just because I want there to be absolutely no barriers between our naked bodies doesn't mean she feels the same. I can't make her feel uncomfortable in her new home.

Rachel bites her lip. "Or…"

"Or?" My heart thumps loudly in my chest. She can't be insinuating what I want her to be. Can she?

"Never mind," she says, shaking her head.

Before I can second guess myself, I set my hand on her knee. "Or what?"

She takes a deep breath. "There's another way we could relax," she says. She sets her hand on top of mine.

My skin prickles where she's touching me, little pinpricks of electricity flooding my veins as blood rushes to my groin. My heart starts to beat a little faster, and my stomach flutters at the sensation of her soft palm on mine.

"Oh?" My voice cracks.

Rachel still looks nervous. "Can we head back to the apartment?"

"Yes. Absolutely." I clear my throat. "Your friend, does she need a ride home?"

She pulls out her phone, sending a text. It buzzes a few moments later with a response.

"She's good. Robby will drive her."

"Great. Let's head out."

As we exit the VIP section, my hand settles on the small of her back. To my surprise, Rachel leans into me, her arm sliding around my waist. My cock jerks in my suit pants at the simple touch.

Okay. So maybe *I* need to relax, too.

seven

. . .

Rachel

AM I REALLY DOING THIS?

I try to look at this clinically. I'm a single woman with needs. Jake is a single man, he's incredibly good-looking, and for some reason, he keeps looking at me like he's undressing me with his eyes. He may have flirted with Viv, but his eyes kept coming back to me.

I can totally have casual, no-strings-attached sex with my ex's brother who's giving me a place to stay. Right?

Leaving aside the fact that I've never been able to have casual, no-strings-attached *anything* before.

Right now, I don't even care if this is a bad idea. I'm so far wound up, I'm about to spring out of my skin like a jack-in-the-box. Watching Jake dominate on the ice was a serious turn-on. I didn't realize how hot it would be to watch him do the thing he's best at.

Snow starts to fall as we make our way to the car, and I huddle deeper into my coat and then squirm closer to Jake. He wraps his arm around me like he doesn't want to let me go.

For one night, I can pretend he likes me for real. For one

night, I can pretend I'm not just another warm body to him. For one night, I can pretend I'm okay.

Inside the car, he cranks the heat and then sets his hand halfway up my thigh. His long, thick fingers dance along my inseam, tapping out a beat.

Heat ricochets through me, settling deep inside my core. I want this, want him. I can't kid myself. Jake is gorgeous. I may have scoped out his Instagram, doing a deep dive. He doesn't post photos with women.

That's okay. I'm okay being anonymous. I'm okay being in his life without it being broadcasted to the entire world. He's letting me into his house. I get to see the real him, unfiltered. That's enough for me.

When we pull into the parking garage, Jake gets out and opens the door for me, then takes my hand in his. The ride up the elevator to the apartment is silent. His calloused palm feels good pressed up against my skin.

I'd like it even more on my bare skin—in other places.

Inside the apartment, he hesitates. "We should set ground rules," he says. "Parameters."

My eyebrow arches up. "Okay?"

"What do you want?"

That's a loaded question.

I want to feel like myself again. I want to feel safe and secure. I want to know who I am and what I need—out of a partner, out of life.

But mainly... I want to get out of my head.

"I want to feel something," I tell him. "Something that isn't apathy or regret. I want to feel like myself again."

He shucks his coat, laying it over his arm before moving to help me out of mine. He hangs them side by side in the front entry closet.

"I can do that," he says. "I don't want to make things uncomfortable for you."

"You're not."

"Whatever happens…" He takes a breath. "It has no bearing on your staying here. You can stay as long as you'd like. I meant it—the room is yours, as long as you want it."

"Thanks." I start to unbutton my shirt. "Are we doing this?"

Jake tilts his head, watching me. "You're kind of intense. You know that?"

Heat rises to my cheeks. "I've heard that before."

"I like it," he says.

Rolling my eyes, I look away. He might say that now, when he's trying to get laid, but he can't actually mean it.

He steps closer, one hand on my chin, tilting my face up until my eyes meet his.

"I like it," he says again. "It's part of why I had such a big crush on you growing up."

My eyes widen. "What?"

He lifts a shoulder in a shrug. "I thought you were pretty freaking fantastic back then. I knew it would never happen— age difference aside, you were way out of my league, still are —but I could dream. So now, you standing here in front of me… I like that you're intense. I like that you're passionate. I like that you're *you*."

"Jake…"

"I can't offer you much," he says. "I know we live very different lives. *I get that.* But just for now, can't we pretend? Can't we just live in the moment?"

Slowly, I nod.

"Thank fuck," he declares. His hand slides from my chin to the back of my head, threading his fingers through my hair, before his lips descend on mine.

Jake devours me, confident and sure. My lips part on a sigh and he surges between them, his tongue licking into my mouth.

My body sways toward him. He hauls me up against him, his hard muscles pressed against my soft curves sending delicious sensations through me. Tiptoeing my fingers up his solid chest, I reach for his tie, pulling it loose. He lets out a soft groan against my lips.

I start to undo his buttons. I get halfway down his torso before he grunts and breaks the kiss, pulling my hand away.

Taking a step back, I swallow. His taste lingers on my lips.

"Should I not?" My voice comes out breathy.

In response, Jake reaches for me, hauling my size twenty-six body over his shoulder. The world tilts upside down, giving me an excellent view of his ass in those suit pants. I grab one cheek. It's rock hard.

"Careful, Rach," he says, his voice hoarse as he walks me through the hallway and down toward his bedroom.

"Or what?" I taunt back.

His hand cups my ass through my jeans, squeezing and kneading the soft flesh there. "Tit for tat, babe."

"You haven't even seen my tits yet."

Jake lays me out on his bed, looming over me. "Patience," he says. He leans down to take off my boots, pulling the shoe free and tossing it behind him before divesting me of my sock, then doing the same to the other foot.

"I don't want to be patient." My hand slips down to the front of my jeans, popping the button.

He hisses between his teeth, reaching for me. He pulls me to the edge of the bed and then undoes my fly, pulling my jeans off my hips.

It's almost time to go for another wax, the hair has grown in on my legs and on my bikini line, but with the way he's looking at me, I don't think he cares. His fingers curl into fists at his sides, his chest rising and falling rapidly.

Slowly, carefully, he exhales. His hands flex.

And then, his eyes on mine, he reaches for the thin band of my panties. They're basic cotton, black with a subtle pink floral pattern.

My breath catches at the hungry look in his eyes. He peels

my panties down my legs and brings them to his nose, inhaling deeply. My face heats.

"Fuck, Rachel," Jake says, his deep voice gravelly. "You smell so good."

I let my legs fall open with a sudden burst of confidence. "Oh? Why don't you give it another check?"

He growls as he falls to his knees in front of me. He tosses my legs over his shoulders before he slides his hands under my ass.

And then he buries his face in my pussy.

I call out at the first touch of his tongue to me. He's ruthless, relentless, devouring me. His tongue slides through my folds as his fingertips dig into the flesh of my ass. Jake brings one hand to my core, gathering the wetness there before slowly sliding a finger inside me.

Immediately, I clench around it. I want more. I *need* more.

He gets me used to the intrusion, thrusting his finger inside of me as his tongue flicks against my clit, sending a maelstrom of pleasure through me.

My hands fall to his thick, dark hair, threading my fingers through the curly strands. Oral is one of my favorite ways to get off, but I haven't found a partner who is both willing and good enough at it.

Jake? He knows what he's doing. And while I feel a tinge of frustration that he's clearly done this before with other women, I'm placated by the fact that he's here with *me*, and I'm the one benefiting from his experience. They're not here in this bed. It's just the two of us.

But how long can that last?

eight

. . .

Jake

SOMETHING IS WRONG, because Rachel doesn't seem into this anymore.

Nipping at her thigh, I pull back. "Where's your head?"

"I'm sorry," she says, carding her fingers through my hair.

"Nothing to be sorry for. What can I do differently?"

She blinks at me.

"Open and honest conversation is the only way this will work," I tell her. "We don't know each other well enough yet. I need time to learn your body."

Time that I hope she'll give me.

Now that I've had a taste of her, now that I know the exquisite curves and rolls of her body, I don't know how I'm going to live without it.

It's simple. We're just going to have to do this again, and again, and again, until we get sick of each other. And since that will never happen, I guess it ends when we die.

Yeah. I'm okay with that.

Rachel waves her hand. "I'm just… in my head."

"What can I do to help?" I'm not a mind reader, and as much as I'd like to ignore it, the fact remains that I haven't known her for more than a decade *and* we've never known each other in this way.

That doesn't mean I don't want to. It just means we need to figure this out.

"I just…" She grunts. "I need something different."

Okay. I can roll with that.

Scooping her up, I lay her back against my pillows. Her dark hair splays around her head like a halo, a brilliant contrast against the white linens. Covering her body with mine, I draw a hand through her hair and kiss her.

As much as I'd like this to go farther, I'm totally okay if this is all that happens between us. It doesn't have to end tonight.

Her soft sigh against my lips drags me back to the moment. Her bottom half is bare, her blouse still on. That won't do.

Slowly, with suddenly clumsy fingers, I unhook the buttons from the loops. She arches against me and helps me pull the gauzy fabric away, tossing it somewhere behind me.

Her black bra is barely able to contain the round swells of her breasts. She's definitely full-figured, a delicious mix of curves and rolls that make my cock pulse in my suit pants.

There's a clasp in the center of her bra, and my eyes dart up to hers for consent. Her eyes are hooded, her mouth open. She runs her hand through my hair and I lean into the touch, my own eyes fluttering shut for a moment.

When I center myself, it's with the singular goal of getting her to that peak of pleasure.

Unclasping her bra, it falls to the floor as I get my hands on her glorious tits. The firm swells overflow my palm—and I don't have small hands. Her areolae are a dusky rose, the nipples pebbled tight into the most delicious little peaks.

I can't resist.

Bending down, I take one into my mouth, swirling my tongue around the tight bud.

Rachel moans, wrapping her legs around me. Her hand in my hair directs my head as she needs it, and I lick and suck at her perfect flesh while I knead and massage her other breast. Pinching her nipple, I softly bite down on the other, and she groans, long and loud.

"Jake."

My name is a soft pant on her lips. I want to hear it again, and again, and again.

"I need you to touch me."

Smiling against her breast, I pinch at her nipple, then draw it into my mouth. "I am touching you."

"I need your fingers," she says, arching her back. "Inside me."

Well, that I can do.

As my hand trails down her side, I sear the memory of her softness into my memory. She's got wide hips and a soft tummy, and as my fingers tip-toe across her belly, she flushes and looks away.

"Hey. What's going on?" I draw her attention back to me.

"Nothing. I'm fine," she lies.

"I don't want you to be *fine*," I counter. "I want you to feel good with me."

"I do," Rachel says quietly. She plucks my hand off her belly and moves it down a bit. "I'll feel better if you touch me."

I can't get a read on her. I don't know what's going on with her.

Tracing the seam of her groin, I draw lines where her thigh meets her pelvis. Her breath hitches and she sinks back against the pillows.

"Fucking touch me," she says, but her breathless words counter the demanding tone.

I'll get to the bottom of this. I will.

But for now, I do as the lady desires.

Sliding two fingers inside her tight, wet heat, I bring my

thumb to her clit. Her soft sighs go straight to my cock. I press my free hand against my crotch, trying to calm down.

Thrusting my fingers deep inside her, I set a steady pace before I bring my mouth back to her breast. I give her the attention she deserves, searching until I find the angle that makes her gasp and the pressure that makes her fist the sheets.

"There. Right fucking there," Rachel says, her hips riding my fingers.

Her walls flutter around me and I make sure to do everything exactly the same, giving her exactly what she needs until she collapses onto the bed.

Slowly, I withdraw my fingers from within her and bring them to my lips, sucking her flavor off my skin. My eyes roll back in my head. Fuck, she tastes so good. I could do this forever with her.

I fall onto the bed beside her. I'm still fully dressed and she's fully nude.

After she's had a few moments to catch her breath, Rachel looks over at me. Her dark eyes take in my rumpled shirt and the tent in my pants. She swallows.

"What?" I ask, suddenly self-conscious.

"Why aren't you naked?" she asks.

I duck my head "We hadn't gotten there yet."

If it happens, great. If she changes her mind, I'm good to take care of myself. I'll remember this night for the rest of my life.

She smiles, her eyes softening. "I want you to get naked."

Bossy, demanding Rachel is back. She keeps flickering in and out, like a candle in the wind, trying bravely to stay alight. I keep getting glimpses of the strong, confident woman I know she is. I don't know who or what tried to snuff out her light, but I can guess it was her douchebag ex.

"Naked," she repeats, tugging my shirt from my pants.

Quickly, I pull off my shirt and the suit pants, leaving me in my boxer-briefs.

"We don't have to do anything you're not comfortable with," I warn her.

Will it kill me to stop now? Yes.

Will I hate myself if I make her do something she doesn't want? Also yes.

"I know." Rachel's eyes are bright with mischief as she cups me over my briefs, and my cock leaps beneath her touch. "I'm comfortable. I'm consenting. I want this to happen."

Surging forward, I bring my lips to hers again, tasting her.

Her wandering hands trace over my torso, dipping into my abs, and down further into my boxers. When she wraps her small hand around my dick, giving me a long, slow stroke, I groan, and she smiles against my lips.

"Please tell me you have a condom," she says.

Pulling away, I grab one from the bedside table along with the lube, because there's no such thing as too much lube. At the same time, I pull off my boxers, my cock springing up to slap against my abs.

Rachel lets out a heavy breath.

"What's wrong?" That's never a good sound after taking your pants off with a woman for the first time.

"I want to say something really inappropriate." She lets out a little giggle, covering her face with the back of her hand.

"Tell me." I pull her hand away, linking our fingers together.

She swallows. "I don't know…"

"Rachel. There's nothing you could say that would make me change my mind."

"You and Josh… you're really nothing alike."

Okay. *That* might have done it. My balls start to shrivel up.

"Please tell me you're not thinking about my brother right now." I stare up at the ceiling and want to die. Just like everything else, my asshole brother ruins what could have been a beautiful moment for me and Rachel.

"Just that he was trying too hard to compensate, and you… clearly, you have nothing to compensate for. You've got a lot going on."

"I can't tell if that's a compliment?"

"Oh, yes. A hundred times, yes." She wraps her hand around my cock, giving me a firm stroke and twisting at the head, making me see stars. "You practically live in a locker room. You've seen what other guys are packing. You are— whew."

"We don't look," I lie. We totally look. There are more than a few sword fights and measuring contests in the locker room.

Rach strokes me again. "I won't be able to look you in the face anymore, not now that I know what you're walking around with."

Tipping her chin up, I meet her eyes. "I want you to look me in the eyes."

"But—"

"This doesn't change anything," I tell her firmly. "We can still be… whatever we are. This doesn't make things awkward or uncomfortable unless we let it."

She swallows.

"Okay?"

She nods. "Okay. Will you fuck me now?"

With a smile, I drop a kiss to her nose before I release her. Grabbing the condom, I suit up quickly and add some lube before I move toward her. I thrust my slicked fingers inside her tightness, adding some additional wetness to make this easier for both of us.

Moving over her, I notch the head of my dick at her entrance. My every sense is heightened, my heart pounding so fast I think I might pass out.

And as I slowly thrust inside, I see heaven for the first time.

Rachel sucks in a deep breath and goes still, so I do, too. She might need time to adjust. Truthfully, I need it just as much. I'm on the edge of embarrassing myself right now. Reaching behind me, I squeeze my balls, gently pulling on my sac to distract me.

Her pussy is tight and hot and wet, clenching around me. She blows out a breath and her muscles relax enough that I don't feel like I'm going to blow my load before this even gets started.

I draw her leg over my hip, opening her up for me. She reaches for me, wrapping her arms around me and running her hands over my back. Her mouth finds mine again, her tongue slipping into my mouth and she takes what she wants.

I'm hers. Whatever she wants, I'm hers.

Pulling back, I thrust into her tight heat, setting a steady pace. Her little mewls of pleasure send electricity through my veins, urging me on. I'll do whatever I need to make these noises come from her lips.

Her hips cradle mine, wide and thick, the perfect place for me. I try out different angles, trying to find what she needs. Pushing her leg up onto my shoulder, I thrust deep inside of her, and Rachel lets out a long, loud moan.

"There," she pants, her hand going to her clit.

Batting her hand away, I stroke her clit with steady, firm pressure until she breaks. Her walls start to flutter around me. Leaning down, I brush her lips with mine, a ghost of a kiss.

She cries out. Tossing her head back, the long column of her neck is exposed, and I kiss her there, too.

When she relaxes against the mattress, I lower her leg. She has a happy, blissed-out smile on her face. She reaches for me, holding me close to her as she gives me a soft, sated kiss.

My cock throbs with want. I try to stay still, try to adjust, but when she makes those delicious noises, I want to go feral.

Rachel arches her hips, squeezing around me. "You didn't come," she says.

"Was waiting for you," I mumble, before burying my face in her neck.

She cards her hands through my hair, fucking herself on my cock. My cock jerks inside of her, desperate to go on.

"I'm a big girl, Jake," she says. "I can handle it."

Giving her another soft kiss, I find the angle I need. Fucking into her tight, wet heat, I take what she's offering, take what I need.

Pleasure starts at the base of my spine, sending zaps of sensation through me. My entire body is alight with fiery pleasure. With a roar, I let myself finally *let go*.

And when I do? Fireworks.

My cock jerks deep inside of her, filling the condom separating us. I wish there was nothing between us.

Collapsing on the bed beside her, I blindly pull off the condom, tie it off, and deposit it on the nightstand. Reaching for her, I pull her into my arms and press my face into her hair.

"Okay," Rachel says, exhaling heavily.

"Okay?" Is that a performance evaluation?

"We're definitely doing that again," she decides.

The teenager inside of me wants to pump his fists and do a happy dance.

Instead, I say, "Okay," and pull her closer.

She might not know it, but I'll do anything for her.

nine

. . .

Rachel

JAKE IS STILL ASLEEP when I crawl out of his bed around two o'clock in the morning, and his door is closed when I get up and leave for work at eight.

I don't know what to think. A *lot* has happened in the last twenty-four hours. Between moving, the hockey game, and an epic fuck-fest, I don't quite know what to do with myself.

So I bury myself in work. It's almost the end of term, so I'm finalizing the exams I'll set for my undergrads and reviewing the work my grad students are doing in the lab.

When I decided to be a nuclear physicist, I knew I'd be tied to academia to fund my research, but I didn't realize how much the balance tilted toward teaching rather than conducting my own research. I didn't really think it through. The scales will hopefully tilt the other direction as I move up the academia ranks, but there's no guarantee. I don't know if I even want to try to tenure. Probably should have before I spent thirteen years and thousands of dollars pursuing a doctoral degree.

There's a knock on my office door frame, and I look up to see Jake looking delicious in a Grizzlies hoodie, holding two coffee cups.

"Hey," he says, a wide smile on his face.

"Hey. I didn't realize you knew where I worked." I keep my tone carefully neutral so I don't burst into an enormous grin.

In all the years together, Erik never once visited me at work.

Not that Jake and I are *together*. He's a friend. My new roommate. He's not my long-term partner in a committed relationship where I thought we both wanted the same things and I'm being strung along for six years.

Guess I'm still bitter.

When this casual fun with the gorgeous hockey player with incredible stamina is over, I might need to spend some time alone before hopping into another relationship.

"You mentioned you taught at MIT. The nuclear physics department isn't *that* big here," he teases.

It's the largest physics department in the country.

"What are you doing here?" I ask, hiding my smile.

"Our practice facility isn't far from here. Finished up for the day and wanted to see what you were up to." He looks over his shoulder into the hallway, then steps forward and closes the door behind him. "I wanted to make sure we were okay."

"We're good, Jake."

He sets one of the coffee cups on my desk. "You're not weirded out? You're not regretting moving in with me?"

"No. Not at all." I look him over. He's tense, his smile tight. "How about you?"

"Oh, no, I'm great. Totally great," he lies.

Standing, I move around my desk to the set of chairs in front of it. I take one, and he sits awkwardly in the other. I reach for his hand.

"It's okay if you're freaked out," I tell him. "We can talk this through."

He fidgets. "I just—I want to know where we stand."

"I do, too." Last night, I thought it would just be sex. But it's clear for him, it's more than that.

"Listen, what I said—"

My eyebrows go up. "What part?"

Jake flushes beet red.

"Hey. Open and honest communication. That's what you said, right?" I nudge him. "I'm here. I'm not going anywhere."

He takes a breath. "Okay. So. Here's the thing."

Oh. This is the part where he lets me down easy. This is the part where he says he had fun, thanks, but no need to repeat.

I don't think I've ever come that hard in my life. He was relentless, so intensely focused on my pleasure. I've never experienced that kind of single-minded attention in bed.

Now that I know what I've been missing out on, how am I supposed to go on without it?

"Iwanttogoonadate," Jake blurts.

I blink.

I blink again.

"I want to go on a date," he says. "With you."

My stomach drops. "O…kay."

His face falls. "You don't want that."

My stomach churns. I want to. I do. But I also know it's not a good idea, not right now.

"It's not that," I hurry to say. "I just got out of a long, toxic relationship. I don't know that I'm ready to date."

He looks like a kicked puppy.

Because of me. I did that to him.

Jake clears his throat, lifting his chin. "Okay. Cool. Great. I'll ask one of my teammates to find me someone, then."

My eyebrows go up. "Find someone?" What's his hurry?

"The team's holiday party is next weekend," he says, his face still flushed. "We're supposed to bring a date."

Oh.

"So it's a team function. It's not a real date, then."

He pauses. "Yeah. Right. Not a *real* date. Just a thing I have to bring *a* date to."

"Well, in that case…"

His face clears. "You'll come with me?"

I can't believe I'm agreeing to this.

But I can't stand the pain on his face when I said I wasn't ready. I can't stand the thought of hurting him more. I can't stand the idea of not getting to experience what we shared last night.

"It's a date," I finally tell him.

His smile stretches ear to ear. He practically bounces out of his seat.

"Thanks, Rach," he says, leaning over to kiss my cheek.

My face heats, and my heart starts to pound a little faster.

"What's the dress code? What do I wear?"

Jake waves a hand. "Don't worry about that."

My eyes narrow. "I need to know—"

"I've got it handled," he says firmly. "Trust me, just this once."

———

Jake has a game tonight, but unlike last night, he doesn't offer me tickets. I watch it on the enormous flat screen TV, curled up in a blanket I've liberated from his bed. He has a road trip tonight. They're off to New Orleans after the game.

My friend Elsy's best friend Mitch plays for New Orleans. I could totally reach out and suggest we grab dinner and watch the game.

It feels weird, though. Jake isn't *mine*. I don't have any claim to him. It feels wrong to publicly pronounce any ties between us.

Once I find an apartment of my own, I'll be out of his hair. We can go back to being nobody to each other.

Although… I don't know how I'm going to give him up. Whether he wants more or not—and it certainly seems like he does—I don't know that I'm ready to give it to him without losing myself in the process.

I don't know who I am without Erik. I need to learn to stand on my own two feet, first.

When the hockey game ends, my phone buzzes with a text.

Were you watching?

Do you want me to watch?

I bite my lip while I wait for his reply.

Rach, I'd kill to have you at every game.

Okay, so he's not being very subtle.

I wish I didn't have this road trip. I'd much rather be home with you.

Going to snuggle with your roomie? Do you even have a roommate?

My phone lights up with a call.

"Hey," he says, his voice deep and gravelly.

"Hi." I fight back a nervous giggle. I don't know why he makes me so awkward. I feel woefully inexperienced next to him.

"Do you want me to snuggle with Sven?" His voice dances with humor. "I think Vanessa might have a problem with it."

"Oh, I wouldn't want to upset her," I tease back.

"Guess I'll have to snuggle you when I get back."

Exhaling slowly, I close my eyes to center myself. "Yeah.

You might have to."

There's a commotion on the other end of the call.

"Listen, Rach…" He trails off.

"What?"

"My house is yours. You know that," he says. "I want you to stay in my room. Sleep in my bed."

I swallow. "You do?"

"I want to come home to you in my bed."

There's no second guessing. He wants this.

So why does that scare me?

And worse, why does it thrill me?

Maybe because it's moving insanely fast, a voice that sounds like Viv says in my head.

And imaginary-Viv is probably right. There's no way I'm ready for something like what he wants.

I guess the important question is, what do *I* want?

"When do you get back?" I ask.

"Late tomorrow night. Probably close to three o'clock in the morning." He sighs. "It's, what, a four hour flight? Yeah, that sounds right."

"I'll wait up for you," I offer, even though I know I'll be dead on my feet the next day.

"You don't have to," Jake says. "Knowing that you're there, coming home to you… that's all I want."

"Okay," I whisper.

"Yeah?"

"I'll sleep in your bed."

"Good. I'm glad." Another loud noise on the other end. "I've got to go. I just wanted to check in."

"I'm good. I'm here. I'm not going anywhere," I tell him.

He exhales heavily. "Good. That makes me happy."

Against my will, my smile stretches from ear to ear. "Me, too."

We hang up and I putter around the house, putting away my dinner dishes, wiping down the counters, and unpacking one of my three suitcases into the guest room closet.

There. That's a good day's work.

I take a quick shower and crawl into Jake's bed. He must have changed the sheets this morning because it smells fresh and clean with an undercurrent of his cologne. I inhale deeply, enveloped in his scent.

A naughty idea comes to my mind. Reaching for my phone, I check the time. He's probably on the plane to New Orleans already.

With just the bedside light on, casting a dark shadow across the room, I whip off my pajama top and pull the sheets up to cover my chest. I fluff my hair until I get it where I want it.

And then I take a photo.

Me.

Naked.

In Jake's bed.

And before I can second guess myself, I send it to him.

Let's see what he has to say about *that*.

ten

. . .

Jake

"I'M GOING TO DIE," I announce.

Sven looks over at me curiously. "Please don't."

"You don't want me to die? Buddy—" My heart leaps in my chest. He likes me. He really likes me!

"Because then Vanessa will have to do more paperwork, and she hates paperwork," he continues, a hundred percent serious. "So please, for my sake, don't die."

With a sigh, I flop back onto my bed. "I'll try not to, because you asked."

Lifting my phone, I check out the picture again.

Rachel.

Naked.

In my bed.

My cock aches, long and stiff in my sweats, and I curse the fact that I signed up for a roommate. What I would give right now to have the room to myself.

I don't even need all that long. I bet I could take care of things in five minutes, flat.

But I can't very well ask Sven to leave the room. And knowing he'd be outside, waiting to be let in, does a good job at deflating the situation in my pants.

Besides, Vanessa isn't on the road trip. Scott is the Logistics Coordinator for this trip. They alternate who travels, so they both get some rest.

I want to text Rachel, but it's the middle of the night. She needs rest. I bite my fist and look at the photo again.

What am I getting myself into?

Am I ready for this?

I toss and turn all night, and when it's time to head downstairs for team breakfast, I'm no closer to an answer.

"You look like shit," MacGregor says to me as I grab a plate.

"Thanks, asshole. Love you, too."

"Trouble in paradise?"

I glare at him. "What, you ready to gloat?"

He sighs. "No, man. I want you to be happy. That's all I want for the team. If you want to talk about it, I've got a listening ear."

"Thanks." I blow out a breath. "I think I might be rushing it with Rachel, but I don't know if I care. I mean, I *care*. About her."

MacGregor's fuzzy red eyebrows go up. "Okay…"

"She just got out of a relationship. I never thought I'd have a chance with her. You know? She was, like, the accumulation of all of my fantasies come to life. And now she's right here within my reach, and…"

"You don't want to scare her off by coming on too strong," he says slowly.

Letting out a sarcastic laugh, I tell him, "Too late. I asked her out on an actual date and she basically shriveled up and told me to get lost."

He cocks his head. "Yeah, that doesn't sound good."

"I got her to agree to come to the team party with me, but…"

MacGregor freezes. "You what?"

"She's coming to the holiday party."

To my surprise, he smiles and shakes his head. "You're insane."

"Am I, though?"

"You don't even know this chick," he points out. "You're family friends, right? How much do you talk to her?"

"I haven't talked to her. Last time I saw her was about thirteen years ago." That was when she and Josh broke up. Wincing, I add, "She used to date my brother."

MacGregor bursts out laughing. "And now you're going after her?"

"He wasn't good enough for her." I stab moodily at my scrambled eggs. "Even then, I knew she deserved better. I was too young then. But now we're both adults. We're on the same playing field."

"No, you're not."

My eyebrows go up. "What do you mean?"

"Dude, you play in the motherfucking NHL. You're a small-time celebrity." He stares at me like I'm dumb.

"So?"

"So she's—pardon my French—she's a 'commoner,'" MacGregor says with air quotes.

"Fuck off. She's not. She's—"

"She's not used to this lifestyle. It will be a big adjustment for her. You're asking her to give up her life to accommodate yours. She has to give up a piece of herself to support you."

I frown. "Does she really, though?"

"Once people see you together and you publicly announce you're together, yeah, she'll get dragged into the public eye whether you want it or not." He shrugs. "Why do you think so many guys stay single?"

"Oh, so it's not just to trawl for pussy in each city?"

MacGregor cringes. "I mean, yeah, that's part of it. But it's the loss of privacy, too. It's hard living your life with everything open and exposed all the time. The press, social media, they all think they're entitled to every piece of our lives. Sometimes it's nice to keep things quiet."

"You got a girl?" He keeps things pretty close to his chest.

He snorts. "Yeah, no. Not for me."

"A guy, then? No judgment." One of my college team-mates is gay and a guy from my AHL days just came out as bi. I've heard rumors about Robby Andrews, our team's equipment manager, but until he decides to announce anything, I'm not going to pry.

"Nah. Just don't have time for anything," MacGregor denies. "I'm not ready to settle down."

"I don't know that I am, either," I admit. "I just know if I let Rachel walk away, I'll never forgive myself."

"That's your answer, then," he tells me. "Don't live your life with regrets. Go get your girl."

It's a long, exhausting day before I get home. The team won, but it was a hard-fought victory. I let two goals slip by me. It's nothing short of a miracle that the offense was able to score three.

Despite my urgency, the team took forever to load the bus to the airport, and then there were mechanical issues with the plane, making us even more delayed.

I'm dead on my feet when I open my front door. The sight of Rachel's boots beside the console table buoys me, lifting my spirits. Dropping my bags, I all but race to my bedroom.

And there she is.

Fast asleep, her hair spread on my pillows, adorable little snuffling sounds filling the room. A t-shirt—it looks like one of mine—is on the floor beside her fuzzy slippers.

Quickly, I pull off my shirt, leaving me in my sweats.

Just in case…

And when I pull back the covers, revealing her nude form, I kick myself for being overly cautious.

Rachel turns over in her sleep, twitching away from the gap in the blankets.

Dropping my sweats, I crawl into the bed beside her, my heart pounding a thousand beats a minute. There's more adrenaline coursing through my veins than during a shutout game when I'm facing the best sniper in the league.

Calm down, I tell myself. She's just a woman. She's just—

Every fantasy come to life.

She's all I've wanted since I knew how to *want*.

And now she's naked. In my bed.

She squirms closer to me, and I wrap her in my arms and pull her into my chest. Rachel lets out a soft sigh and burrows into my torso, her cheek on my chest.

I could do this forever.

I was dog tired a few moments ago, but now I'm wide awake. I don't know how long this will last. I want to enjoy every fucking moment, sear it into my brain like a brand.

Holding her in my arms, coming home to her... it feels right.

It feels inevitable.

Now I just have to figure out a way to keep her.

eleven

. . .

Rachel

HATTIE GIVES me a knowing look when I enter the office we share. "Have a good night?"

"What are you talking about?"

"You have pash rash."

"What?"

She smirks, pointing at my neck. "Beard burn." Why does she have to sound so damn smug?

Fuck. I clap a hand over my neck. Jake likes to sleep with his face tucked into my neck, like I'm his teddy bear.

"So I guess things are getting better in the post-Erik world."

"I mean... I'm doing okay," I admit.

I don't think about him nearly as often as I used to. I don't want to think about him at all.

Six and a half years, down the drain. When I think about how much mental energy I invested into the relationship, I get angry. He strung me along with no intention of ever taking things further. And because I was young and naive, I thought that's what relationships were supposed to be about —pushing each other, wanting the next step.

And at the same time... my biological clock is ticking.

Every woman in my family has had trouble conceiving on top of early menopause. My time for a biological child without intervention is slowly dwindling. And I know there are other ways to have a baby, there's medical treatments I can try and surrogacy and adoption is always an option… but that's not what I want.

Before I have a baby, though, I want to be married. I want the commitment of a lifetime together. Divorces happen, a ring doesn't mean it is going to last forever, but I want to go into it with the intention of forever.

And to get to the point where I can even *think* about tying the knot with someone, I have to date them first. And to date them, I should probably be fully over my ex first.

"I brought you something," Hattie says.

My eyebrows go up.

She reaches into her desk, pulling out a Dunkin' bag.

Inside are two perfectly beautiful donuts. One is chocolate cream pie, I can tell. It's my favorite. The other is chocolate glazed with colorful sprinkles.

"What's the occasion?" I ask as I pull out the donuts.

I shouldn't. I want to, but I shouldn't.

And then I think of the way Jake looked at my naked body. He likes my curves and rolls. He likes my body.

I take a bite of the donut. It's delicious.

"Felt bad you didn't get one last week at the meeting," Hattie says. "You deserve all the things."

Aww. I give her a hug and she startles before she hugs me back.

We settle at our desks and get some work done. She's teaching in the morning and in the lab in the afternoon, whereas I have grading to do this morning and then teaching this afternoon. I actually can't remember the last time I got uninterrupted time in the lab. My classes haven't changed all semester, but Erik didn't like when I brought marking home to do, so I'd inevitably use up my designated lab time with grading. My grad student TA does a lot of it, but it seems like every time I'm caught up, there's still more that I have to do.

There's a knock on the door around four o'clock. My last class of the day has just wrapped up and I'm trying to get organized for the days ahead.

Jake is in the doorway, wearing another Grizzlies jacket under his open coat.

"What are you doing here?" I ask. Okay, *demand*.

His eyebrows go up. "Should I not be here?"

"I—" I take a breath. "I'm happy to see you, but I wasn't expecting you."

"It's starting to snow," he says.

"It's December. It snows a lot here."

It's the third time in two weeks that he's dropped by my office without warning. I'm starting to think he's inventing reasons to come by.

Jake chuckles. "They're saying a storm is moving in. I didn't want you to have to navigate the T. Figured I'd come pick you up."

Oh. I swallow.

"Thanks." My voice comes out as a whisper.

He crosses the room, then reaches for me and tips my chin up.

"Any time," he says quietly.

My eyes fall closed. He smells fresh, like his Irish Spring soap, and the now familiar scent of his natural pheromones calms me.

His fingers ghost over my cheek. "Rachel…"

Slowly, my eyes blink open. "Yeah?"

Jake grins. "Let's go home."

My mouth goes dry. "O-okay."

I have yet to spend a single night in the bed he designated as mine. From the get-go, he's made clear he likes me in his bed.

Waking up in Jake's arms the last few days has been a

blissful heaven I didn't know existed. I've shared a bed with other guys before, but something about the way he holds me like he doesn't want to let me go makes butterflies erupt in my stomach at the memory.

Last week, he had a day off hockey, so he dropped by the university and we grabbed lunch between administering exams, and when I got home after, he cooked dinner and we watched a movie.

Well. I tried to watch a movie. Every time I glanced over at him, he was watching me.

So I guess it was inevitable that we ended up in bed again, this time with me on my hands and knees as he fucked me senseless.

And the next night, we ate dinner on the couch and then he ate me out until I saw stars.

And the night after that…

We haven't talked about what it means, though.

He drives with his hand on my thigh. The snow is falling more heavily, so sometimes he needs both hands on the wheel, but as soon as he's in a steady place, he's holding me again.

There are groceries in the trunk of the car. Jake doesn't let me help—he manages to carry all six bags at once… though he does let me punch in the code to open the door.

"You went grocery shopping?" I'd have thought a famous hockey player couldn't get to the store without being mobbed.

"They're saying it could turn into a blizzard," Jake says. He starts unloading the bags. He's bought staples like bread and milk, and other things like salmon, chicken breasts, and fresh fruits and vegetables. "We shouldn't lose power, the building is pretty secure, but we might not be able to get out for a few days. They've cancelled practice for the next two days, and the game the day after may be postponed."

"Wow. I hadn't realized." I don't really pay attention to

the weather report. It's cold, it snows, and sometimes there's freezing rain. I walk the two blocks to the nearest T station, I walk from my stop to campus, and then I walk back. I don't really go outside other than that. Even on campus, I eat lunch at my desk rather than trekking to the faculty dining hall.

Jake gives me a small smile. "Guess you're stuck with me for a few days."

"Oh, whatever shall we do," I deadpan.

I start unbuttoning my shirt, and he gulps, his eyes glued to my chest. He shakes his head a few times, as if to clear it, then turns to face the other direction.

My good mood falls. Does he not want to have sex anymore? It was the only thing we had going for us, but if he's not interested and we're trapped together…

As I watch, he shoves food into the cabinets and the fridge, heedless of where things go. He's pretty meticulous about his kitchen organization. He showed me his system on the second day and I've been mindful of putting things in their designated spot.

"Okay, all done," Jake says, stowing the empty bags. "Let's go."

I blink at him. "Go where?" If it turns into a blizzard, I want to be safe in the apartment.

He reaches for me, and before I know what's happening, I'm upside down, tossed over his shoulder like a rag doll. Like the first night, he carries me down the hall, lays me in his bed, and strips me bare. He fucks me sweet and slow, and then hard and fast, and when I come I scream so loud I'm fairly sure they can hear us two floors below.

I could get used to this.

twelve

. . .

Jake

WHEN I WAKE UP, Rachel is gone. So is my t-shirt.

Pulling on a pair of sweats and my slippers, I stretch my arms over my head as I search the small apartment for her. Snow falls steadily outside, and when I look down at the ground twenty stories below us, all I can see is a blanket of white.

She's in the kitchen, wearing my t-shirt and a pair of fuzzy socks and nothing else. As I watch from the doorway, she stirs something in a big mixing bowl. Flour dusts the countertop.

"Whatcha doing?" I ask, leaning against the door frame.

She jumps, and whatever she's stirring jolts, too.

"You scared me," she pouts.

"You were gone."

Crossing the room, I pull her into my arms, and she comes readily, leaning up to kiss me.

"Wanted to make you pancakes," Rachel murmurs.

I pause. "I know we have a break for a few days, but I have to eat fairly clean."

She smiles. "I know. I added protein powder and Greek yogurt to the batter." Reaching for her phone, she shows me the recipe. "Protein pancakes are on your meal plan, right?"

Nodding, I kiss her shoulder. "You looked up a recipe for me?"

Rachel shrugs. "I wanted to make you something. You've done most of the cooking so far."

"I like cooking." It's relaxing. After a long day at practice or in the gym, it's my favorite way to unwind.

Well. My other favorite way would involve the two of us naked in my bed. But she has a life outside of me. I can't ask her to quit her job and stay in my house, ready to be railed at any moment.

I can dream, though.

My arms wrap around her belly and I think of other dreams, too. Maybe one day, a few years from now, we could be standing here with her belly swollen with my baby, making these same pancakes. Sometimes there's a toddler running around the place. Other fantasies have a dog barking in the background and a cat winding it's way between our legs.

One thing is constant: Rachel.

It's soon. It's ridiculously early to have these types of thoughts. I'm afraid to bring them up to her in case she laughs herself out the door.

She's got enough on her plate. She's trying to figure herself out. I can wait. I can be patient.

I kiss her temple as she returns to her pancakes. She's warming chicken sausages in the oven and chopped fruit for a smoothie. She's thought of all my dietary restrictions and planned accordingly.

Fuck, I love this girl.

We eat breakfast at the kitchen bar, her legs over my lap as I feed her berries.

"I was thinking of going home," Rachel says out of nowhere.

My eyebrows go up. "To New Hampshire?"

She nods. "Chanukah starts next week. My mom is alone and, well… it feels like I should go home."

"But do you *want* to?"

She chews her lip. "Not really."

"Why don't you have her come up here? She can stay in the guest room."

Rachel blinks a few times. "The guest room I don't sleep in?"

"Well, yeah."

"And where am I supposed to sleep?"

"My bed."

"Jake, we're not dating," she says gently.

She doesn't have to remind me about it.

"I know." I rub at my chest, trying to take out the sting behind my clavicle. "I can sleep on the air mattress for a few nights."

"You're not going to sleep on an air mattress. I'll do it," she says.

"Rachel—"

"We can figure that out later," she says, waving it away. "Why do you want my mom to come visit?"

"You miss her. You want to see her."

She nods slowly. "And I can go home."

"You don't have a car. How would you get home?"

"I'd take the Greyhound."

"No." I shake my head.

"No?" Her eyebrows go up. "You don't get to say whether I do or don't do *anything*," she snaps.

I take a breath to cool down. "I'd drive you, or I'd get Jeremy to come down and drive you back," I tell her. "I don't want you taking some sketchy bus."

She relaxes. "I don't want to take a sketchy bus, either. I'm a grown-up. I can deal with it."

"I don't want you to *deal with it*. I want you and your mom to have a fun weekend in the city. You can get a massage and go out to the theater and all sorts of things." That's what my mom likes to do when she visits the city. I'm guessing her mom likes similar.

Rachel cocks her head, staring at me.

"Why don't we invite my parents, too? We can make it a little Chanukah party."

Her eyes go wide. "You want to invite *your parents*?"

"And your mom." Her dad passed a few years ago and she's an only child. "My brothers, too."

She shifts. "What about Josh?"

"Yeah, he's one of my brothers…" I study her face. "Does that make you uncomfortable? Seeing him again?"

"No, I don't care about him," she says, and I believe her. She waves a hand. "Just that if we're…"

My eyebrows go up. "If we're what?"

She swallows and straightens her shoulders. "If we're going to continue sleeping together," Rachel says bluntly, "We'll have to tell him. Especially before he comes to visit."

"Do you want to keep sleeping together?" I don't know that I want to know the answer. I mean, I do, but only if it's going to be a yes. I don't want there to be any other option.

She takes a breath. "I'd like to, yes," she says. Her eyes flick up to mine and then away. "I'm not ready for more."

"Am I pushing you for more?" It's an honest question. I really don't think I am. Maybe I'm doing something subconsciously.

"You're not," Rachel says. "I know you want more, but you've respected that I'm not able to give it." She exhales heavily. "I'm working on myself. I want to get to a place where I can be open to more. I'm just not there yet."

"There's no rush," I tell her, taking her hand. "When we have forever ahead of us, a little bit of time is easy to give."

She gulps. "Forever?"

"That's what I want. Forever. With you."

Rachel goes tense.

"But I know you're not ready, I'm okay with taking it a day at a time," I'm quick to add.

"One day at a time," she agrees.

———

Snow falls steadily over the next few hours. Because we're so high up, we can see the snowfall swirling around us and dropping to the street below. We're well and truly snowed in.

After we clean up the breakfast dishes, we take showers—separately—and curl up on the couch. Rachel puts on a Chanukah Hallmark movie and I make hot cocoa for both of us, with plenty of marshmallows for her.

"I can't believe you're watching this," she comments as she lays on my chest, my hand threaded though her hair.

"Why?"

"I thought you'd want to watch sports replays or an action movie."

Laughing, I kiss her temple. "Way to stereotype."

She's not wrong.

But when the alternative is holding her in my arms? Yeah, I'll do whatever she wants.

After the movie ends, I pull out the box that lives in my linen closet. I don't have a lot of holiday decor. I have more flamingo summer decorations than Chanukah.

Rachel takes my phone and opens the online shopping app. Together, we scroll through the site. She picks garlands to hang in front of the mantle and a set of Chanukah gnomes that I kind of want to display year round. There's a frosted winter gingerbread-style house with a menorah in the front window. I have a menorah already, so she one-clicks on candles to fill it.

I never would have thought I'd need this. As soon as I see her eyes light up, we add it to the cart. Whatever she wants, we add it to the cart.

We spend two days on the couch, buried under a pile of blankets. We make out, take breaks for snacks, and play cards and board games. She cheats. Blatantly. Every time.

And I let her, like the lovesick fool I am.

When the snow starts to clear and the impromptu vacation comes to an end, I'm almost sorry. Does it suck to have missed a game? Yes. I love playing, and I'll happily do it every chance I get. But these last few days... I wouldn't change them for the world.

thirteen

. . .

Rachel

TWO DAYS after the world goes back to normal, tonight is the team's holiday party. I texted Vanessa about the dress code and she was much more helpful than Jake was. I think I have a dress figured out.

She also suggested we get our nails done together. I'm sure she's dying for the gossip. I've been holding out on my friends. Aside from a quick text in the group chat that I found a place to stay, I've been keeping a low profile. I even skipped our monthly Neurospicy Book Club meetup.

I'm sure my friends want to make sure I'm okay, but sometimes their concern is smothering. It's one of many reasons I stopped couch surfing and agreed to stay here. They mean well. They love hard. I'm just not always good at accepting their love.

It's a common thread in my life.

Jake wanders into the kitchen, his hair mussed from sleep. He's wearing a pair of gray sweats—and nothing else.

"Morning," he says, reaching me and kissing my cheek. He pulls me into his arms and I wrap mine around his neck. He smells good, his fresh Irish Spring scent comforting me.

"Mm. Morning." I offer him a sip of my coffee, but he shakes his head.

"Let's go back to bed. Let's spend the entire day naked," he says.

With a laugh, I pull back. "You have practice. And I have plans."

"Oh. Yeah." He heads toward the coffee maker, then pauses. "Plans?"

"I'm meeting Vanessa."

He gives me a faint smile, his eyes bright. "I like Van. She's cool."

"I'm glad you approve," I say dryly.

Secretly, I am glad he likes my friends. It would make this infinitely more difficult if they didn't get along.

Jake makes us both breakfast and we sit at the kitchen counter elbow to elbow. It's nice, having someone at my side.

After I do the dishes—it's only fair since he cooked—I go to get ready for my nail appointment and he gets dressed for practice. We head out the door at the same time.

"Oh, here," Jake says, reaching into his pocket. He pulls out his wallet and offers me a credit card.

I don't take the card. "What's this for?"

"For your nails," he says.

I stare up at him. "I can pay for my own nails."

"Yeah. But I want to treat you," he says.

"I'm a big girl. I don't need your money," I tell him.

"I know you are. And I know you don't," Jake says evenly. He inhales sharply. "I want to do something nice for you. Will you please let me pamper you?"

With a sigh, I relent. He's clumsy about it, but he's being sweet. He has good intentions.

"Thank you," I whisper.

He tips my chin up. "I just want to take care of you," he says. "I want to make you happy."

"You don't have to buy me things to make me happy. I just want you."

Jake brushes a kiss against my lips. "Me, too."

Leaning down, he pushes his card into the side pocket of my leggings.

"I'll be back around two," he says.

He offers to drive me to the nail salon, but I insist on taking the T across town. Once I'm on the subway car, though, surrounded by the stifling heat and the stench of body odor, I start to regret it.

He's genuinely kind and thoughtful, if a bit heavy-handed with it. We can work on this.

Vanessa is waiting for me at the nail salon with Hailey MacGregor.

"Hey," Van says, giving me a warm hug. "You know Hailey, right?"

"We met the other night." I give the woman a brief hug and she returns it readily.

"Awesome. I'm trying to recruit more normal people to the club," Van says.

My eyebrows go up. "The club?"

"Yeah. Attached to the players, but not necessarily part of the WAG lifestyle."

"I love Melanie," Hailey adds. "She's just… a lot."

"And a lot of the other girlfriends don't like that I work for the team," Van adds. "They think I should give up my job and flit around the city all day. Look, I love Sven, but even after we're married, I'm still going to keep my job."

I glance at her hand. There's no ring there.

"We're not in a rush." She sounds defensive, crossing her arms over her chest.

"Hey, I get it," I tell her. "I thought I was on the conveyor belt to marriage and babies until it suddenly collapsed. I get not wanting to rush into things."

Sometimes I wish I'd forced the issue with Erik. If I'd

given him an ultimatum, it would have been the end of things either way, because that's not a basis for a healthy relationship. Who knows where I would have been if I'd walked away from him two years in, rather than spending six and a half years waiting on a "maybe soon."

"Is that what you still want? Marriage and babies?" Hailey asks.

"I haven't let myself think about it, honestly," I tell her. "Jake isn't—"

Her eyebrows go up. "He isn't *what*?"

"I don't know if he's the kind of guy who wants marriage and babies." I shrug. "Right now, we're just having fun. I'm still getting over my ex. We're keeping things casual."

She looks me up and down, clearly not believing me. "He's bringing you to the party tonight. He is *not* keeping things casual."

I pause. "What does that mean?"

"He likes you. He really likes you," Hailey says. Why does she sound upset? "If this is just a passing thing for you—"

I have to ask. "Do you have feelings for Jake?"

There's a hollow feeling in the pit of my stomach. I feel vaguely sick.

To my surprise, Hailey laughs. "No. He's like a brother to me. He hangs out with Aidan and Sven a lot, so I'd say I know him fairly well. He's a goofy, kind-hearted, over-grown man child. But when he loves, he loves hard."

"I want to love him," I whisper. "It's just... it's too soon."

"Is it, though?" Van cocks her head. "I thought it was too soon for me and Sven. He's in this for the long haul, but he's made it clear the timeline is up to me. Can't it be the same for you and Jake?"

Biting my lip, I think it over.

"Does it have to end in marriage and babies?" Hailey asks. "Can you be happy if it ends up with you in a committed partnership without the ceremony?"

"I don't want or need a ring or a fancy party," I tell her. "I just want the commitment."

She points at me. "Now all you have to do is talk to Jake. Make sure you're on the same page."

As if it's that easy…

And when I get back to the apartment and find a black carrier bag from a designer boutique in it and pull out a gorgeous sequined dress in just my size… I think it might be.

fourteen

. . .

Jake

WHEN RACHEL WALKS out of her bedroom, my jaw hits the floor.

"Holy fuck."

Her cheeks flush. "Should I change?"

Rising from the couch, I make my way over to her. I take her hand and brush my thumb over the back of her knuckles. "No. Never change."

After MacGregor's jawing about the party, I decided to treat her right. Larsson gave me the name of the boutique where he buys Vanessa presents and I had a dress and shoes delivered. I wanted to suggest she get her hair and makeup done after her nail appointment, too, but I didn't want to overstep. I don't want to change her or dress her up like a doll. I just want her to feel good in her skin.

At least Hailey convinced her to get a massage after their nails. She deserves to be pampered.

She deserves the world.

And looking at her now, wearing a floor-length sequined gown with a deep dip in the front, clinging in all the right places, her hair done and her makeup emphasizing her features…

She takes my breath away.

I swallow hard.

"You look… amazing," I manage around the lump in my throat.

Rachel looks away, and my finger on her chin forces her eyes up to meet mine.

"You look amazing," I repeat. "I'm torn between staying here all night and taking you out on the town and showing you off."

"It's just… hair. And makeup." She waves a hand. "It's nothing."

Do I like her done up? Yeah.

I also like her fresh-faced, no makeup, wearing old, worn sweatpants and my t-shirt. I like her wearing her blazers and blouses for work. I like her naked and sweaty in my bed.

Basically, I just like her. The hair and makeup is just gift wrap on top of the present.

She brushes some invisible lint off my shoulder. "I like the suit."

I've chosen a dark, navy blue suit with a blue and white checked shirt and a dark yellow tie. I wear suits all the time—every time I head to the arena, it's a suit, required by the league. I was never a clothes-hound until I got into the league. Then it seemed like all the guys were into suits and fashion, fast cars, and golf. I still have no interest in golf. Two out of the three ain't bad.

Tonight, I've put thought into my outfit, coordinating with her navy blue sequined dress. I want us to look like two pieces of a matching set rather than two people haphazardly thrown together. Like it or not, she owns me. And I like it. I like it a lot.

We make our way down to the garage and I open the door for her. Before, I was hesitant about touching her, too nervous about upsetting her or making her uncomfortable.

Now, though, my hand sits on her knee like it belongs there.

She tells me about her day, about seeing Van and getting to know Hailey better. She even suggested Hailey join their book club. I'm glad she's getting along with my friends.

Sometimes I think it's a little weird that MacGregor brings Hailey along to events where he would otherwise need a date. He doesn't date at all.

But when I think about them losing their parents young and how he basically raised her, plus her medical fragility, it makes sense that he wants to keep her close. They're best friends, peas in a pod.

It's still weird that she's here as his date, though.

The steakhouse's back room is decked out in Christmas decor. Easton gives me an up-nod as I enter the room, and to my surprise, Melanie greets Rachel with a warm hug. I hadn't realized they'd gotten so close after the game the other night.

I feel like a million bucks with her on my arm tonight. She's the most gorgeous woman in the room.

We stop at the bar for a drink—she opts for water, so I do, too—and make a lap of the room. Almost all of the guys have brought a date. A few of the young rookies, like Henry and Jenkins, have wide-eyed expressions like they can't believe they're here.

The team throws these big parties all the time. There's the start of season banquet, the Halloween party, the Thanksgiving family feast, the holiday party... there will be a New Year's Eve bash, too, plus a big party before the All Star break.

It's a *lot*.

Rachel keeps to my side, letting me hold her hand or put my hand on the small of her back as we mingle and chat. She brightens when we reach Larsson and Vanessa, a genuine smile on her face.

He's my roommate on the road, my buddy and my teammate, but we don't hang out much outside of work. I have a feeling that's about to change. I want to make her feel like she's part of my life because if I have my way, she will be.

"What are you doing this weekend?" Van asks. "There's a craft fair in Marblehead I was thinking of checking out.

Rachel hums. "I'm heading to New Hampshire for the weekend."

My eyebrows go up. "You are?" I thought we decided she would stay here.

She shrugs. "I have two weeks off of work, but I don't really want to stay the whole time. About seventy-two hours in my hometown is all I can handle."

"I thought your mom was coming down." I shove my hand into my pocket to hide the tremor. Why am I shaking?

"Just for a bit." Rachel lifts her shoulder easily. "I need to get back to looking for an apartment."

My jaw clenches as I try not to grit my teeth. "You're staying with me."

"Yeah, for now," she says with a laugh. "I can't stay there forever."

"Why not?" Holy fuck, I sound like a petulant child, whining about getting his favorite toy yanked away.

Rachel's eyes dart to Sven and Vanessa. "Maybe we shouldn't talk about this here."

I clear my throat. "Excuse us."

Grabbing her hand, I pull her into an alcove. Hidden by the shadows, I feel comfortable enough to bare my soul.

"I told you I want you to stay with me," I tell her.

"And I said I would," Rachel says. She sets her jaw. "What's going on with you?"

"I want you. I want us. I thought I was clear about that."

"And I thought I was clear that I'm not ready for that." Her lip trembles. "Look, I like you. I do."

"But..." My stomach falls.

"But I just got out of a serious, long-term relationship

where he treated me like shit for most of that time," Rachel says. "I'm not in a headspace where I can dive into something new. I don't want you to be a rebound."

"You can use me as a rebound. That's fine. I don't care," I lie.

She shakes her head, cupping my face. "*I* care. I can't do that to you."

"So the last two weeks, our snow days..." Coming home to her every night, spending each evening together, fucking and then sleeping together... it's been incredibly intimate. I've never let someone into my life the way I have with her.

"It's been great. But it can't last," Rachel says. "It's not real life."

"It can be whatever we want it to be." I feel like I'm grasping at straws, desperately trying to hold onto someone determined to slip through my fingers.

She gives a hollow laugh. "Girls like me don't end up with guys like you."

"What do you mean?" Giving into the urge, I pull her into my arms. "Girls way out of my league?"

"Jake. You're a hockey player."

"So?" Does my being an athlete turn her off?

"So you can get all the women you want. You don't want a fat, frumpy physicist when you could—"

"I want *you*," I tell her firmly. "I could tell you until I'm blue in the face that I like the way you look and the way you dress. I *love* that you went after what you want until you got your Ph.D. I am so incredibly proud of you for achieving that."

She swallows.

"I've always been interested in you. Why do you think I offered you the room?"

"Because..." She shakes her head. "I don't know."

"Like you said, I'm a professional athlete. I don't need a roommate."

Rachel looks away.

"I *want* to share my space with you. I want you to be there. I want you to be part of my life." I tip her chin up. "I want you. Whatever you can give me. If all we have is a brief moment in time before you move on, I still want it."

I can find a way to be happy with the scraps she can give. I'd rather have whatever she can offer than nothing at all.

"You'll get tired of me," she says. "I'm boring. I don't—"

"You're not boring," I interrupt.

She laughs. "You don't even know me. Not really."

"Okay. So tell me what I need to know."

"I'm a stay-at-home type person. I don't like to go out to bars and clubs."

"Cool. Neither do I."

Rachel laughs again. "You took me to a bar after your game."

"Because you were a guest, and that's what we do with guests." I shrug. "Easton doesn't go to the bars. MacGregor, almost never. I wanted you to have the VIP hockey experience. No skin off my back if we don't go again."

She opens her mouth.

"I want to spend time with you. That doesn't mean I don't have other interests or friends," I tell her. "I spend plenty of time with the guys on the road and at practice. We hang out all the time. When it's all over? I want to come home to you."

fifteen

. . .

Rachel

WHY AM I FIGHTING THIS? I want to like Jake. I want to let myself fall for him.

But I've been burned too many times. I've lost myself in too many guys.

It starts out small. A little corner edge here. A crease there. A tiny rip. And then the tears start getting bigger. Huge chunks get ripped away.

I don't know who I am right now. I'm barely able to stand on my own two feet. I have a steady job, I can pay my way, but I don't have the safety net I once did.

And Jake can't be my safety net. I need to find it on my own.

"I want to be there when you come home," I finally tell him. "But I also need to be an equal. I won't be less than because you have more money and more power."

"I have no power," Jake says, lifting a hand.

I snort.

"I am utterly powerless when it comes to you," he says quietly.

My stomach swoops. I want to believe him. *I do*. He's saying all the right things.

"Rach, all I've wanted is you. Knowing you in this way… it's a privilege. I don't take it lightly."

His rich brown eyes are telling me the truth, I know it deep in my soul.

So why is it so hard to trust him?

"If you meet a woman who—"

"Not interested," he interrupts.

"I'm just saying. If you meet someone…"

"If I meet someone, I'd say, there's no way she could compare to you." He cups my cheek. "I don't care what she looks like or what size dress she wears or how many advanced degrees she has. *She's not you.*"

My heart pounds wildly in my chest. "Jake…"

"I know we just reconnected. I know it's too soon," he says. "The way I feel for you? That's not going to go away."

"It's just a honeymoon phase. All relationships start out this way." I chew my lip.

"Maybe. I know my own mind. And this deep, soul-crushing way I feel about you? That's not a phase. That's real."

I swallow against the lump in my throat. "But…"

"I'm in this, Rach," he says. "For however long you'll let me, I'm in. If you want to walk away tomorrow, yeah, I might be devastated. But it would still be better than not ever having a chance with you."

"Come home with me," I blurt. "Come to New Hampshire."

He gives me a crooked smile. "You want me to come meet your mom?"

"I do." My heart flutters. "Yeah, I do."

"You wouldn't do that if you didn't want to keep me," he rationalizes as he pulls me into his arms.

"I want to keep you," I tell him. "I don't know how I'm going to manage it. I just know I want it."

His smile stretches from ear to ear. "Say it again."

"I want you," I whisper.

Jake reaches for me, or maybe I reach for him, or maybe we both do. We meet in the middle for a desperate kiss. His tongue slips between my lips, tasting me, devouring me. I pull him close, my eager hands covering his shoulders and his chest and his perfect washboard abs.

I have no idea how I'm going to make this work. I don't want him to be a rebound; he deserves better than that.

I do know I'm going to give it my all. He deserves that, too.

A throat clears, and I pull back to see an older guy in a suit staring disapprovingly at us. He's maybe early forties with a touch of gray in his beard. He's hot, in an objective way.

But he can't compare to my guy.

"Lewis," he says. He nods at me. "Hi."

"McKittrick." Jake's voice is gravelly and deep. "What do you want?"

To my surprise, McKittrick's poker face falls into a massive shit-eating grin. "Congrats. Not the time or the place, dude. Congratulations either way."

My face heats. I almost forgot we were at this party. I definitely forgot we were in public.

Jake hugs me against his chest. "Thanks. Now leave us alone."

McKittrick laughs. "Yeah, no. It's time to sit down for dinner."

Peering around him, I do notice people starting to take their seats.

"I'm Jason," he says, offering me a hand.

"Rachel," I introduce.

"McKittrick is our captain. He's basically our team dad," Jake says. He cocks his head. "Do women call you Daddy?"

"Fuck you," McKittrick says with a grin. He turns to me. "Can I escort you to the table?"

Jake's booming laugh echoes in my ear. "Not a chance."

Taking our seats at one of the tables, we're surrounded by Sven and Vanessa, MacGregor and Hailey, and McKittrick and Logan, who didn't bring dates. I'm introduced to Henry, the other half of the goaltending tandem, and Jenkins, a second-year player that Jake's mentioned briefly as a bit of a wildcard.

These are his people. His family. He's including me, bringing me into his life.

Jake's arm is wrapped around my shoulders as Coach Turner and ownership give speeches. He releases me only when it's time to eat our meals.

After, when the tables are cleared, we move to the dance floor. He's not shy about pulling me into his arms, holding me close even through the fast-paced, upbeat songs. We're attracting some attention. He doesn't let it bother him, so I don't, either.

Reaching for him, I cup his cheek. Jake looks down at me with such earnestness in his eyes, it brings tears to mine.

"Hey. What's going on?" He wipes his thumb beneath my eye.

"We're doing this." I still can't believe it. "We're really doing this."

He leans down and brushes a soft kiss against my lips. "Yeah. We're doing this."

Except after a few hours, I'm starting to flag. Parties like this are fun in theory, but after a little while, I just get so overwhelmed all I want to do is curl into the fetal position in my bed.

Jake can keep going all night. That's one of the perks of being twenty-six, I guess. When I was twenty-six, I was knee-deep in doctoral research, so I didn't have much time for partying.

We truly live such different lifestyles. I still can't believe he's interested in anything to do with me.

But when he looks at me and suggests we head out... I don't want to go anywhere without him.

Snow falls more heavily on our drive home. What should take twenty minutes is closer to forty-five. Roads are cordoned off and traffic is heavier than usual for midnight. I'm very glad all I have to do is mark some exams before my two weeks off.

"Looks like a storm is coming," Jake says as he pulls into the parking garage. "Do you want me to drive you to campus tomorrow?"

"I'll be fine," I tell him.

He's out of the car in an instant, hopping around to open my door for me.

"I didn't ask if you would be fine. I asked if you wanted me to drive you."

Oh.

"All I have is practice, I can drop you off, head to the rink, and swing by to pick you up after."

I have to lean in. I have to trust myself—and him.

"That would be nice. Thank you."

Jake grabs my hand and kisses the back of my knuckles. "It's my pleasure."

sixteen

. . .

Jake

CLOTHES GO FLYING. My suit jacket lands in a crumpled heap, my pants get shoved down, and I think one of my shoes dents the wall.

I don't care. Scooping Rachel into my arms, I stride confidently toward the bedroom.

Her sequined dress zips halfway up her back, and as I slowly drag the tab down, I hear her swallow loudly.

"Jake…"

I pause. "Rach."

She turns. "I should do it," she says.

"Do what?"

Her pale cheeks flush red. "I'm wearing a bodysuit."

I squint at her. "Like a superhero?"

She laughs weakly. "No. Like… to hold everything in."

"Is that a bad thing?"

She swallows again. "I just… I don't want you to see it and get turned off."

"Trust me, that won't happen."

"But—"

"Trust me, Rach, I *like* your body exactly the way it is." I pinch her hip. "I don't care what you are or aren't wearing under your dress."

She reaches for the zipper of her gown, then lets it pool to her feet. She's left in a spandex bodysuit that covers her from chest to knees.

It does hold in her curves. It gives her more of a snatched-in look. But I don't like her better this way. It doesn't change the way I feel about her body.

Cupping her cheek, I kiss her slowly. "I want you naked." My voice comes out raspy and hoarse.

She reaches behind her, slowly unfastening the body suit. Her movements are decidedly not graceful. It almost looks like she's struggling against the spandex.

Finally, she gets the material off her hips, then steps away. She's fully nude in front of me, her glorious curves and rolls on display, and my cock twitches. I stroke myself slowly to take the edge off.

Rachel looks up at me from beneath her lashes, her face pink. "So…"

Stepping forward, I crush my mouth to hers, trying to wordlessly show her all the ways I want this. I'm in this.

Backing her slowly toward the bed, I twist so I land on my back, then pull her on top of me. She straddles me, her knees keeping her weight off of me.

Yanking her down, I pull her onto my lap until her wet, hot core rests against my bare cock. She lifts up and rolls her hips before sinking down against me.

I pant against her mouth. She's going to drive me insane.

Rachel breaks the kiss, breathing hard. I run my hand through her hair. It was curled earlier, but now it's mostly straight again, soft and shiny from the product in it.

Burying her face in my neck, her teeth graze my skin, and my cock jerks against her.

So she does it again, the little minx.

She sucks on the sensitive spot beneath my jaw, blooming

a mark there. And then she kisses her way down my neck, sucking on the hollow of my throat. Her hands touch me everywhere her mouth isn't, stroking my pecs, dancing in the divots between my abs.

As much as I'm in a hurry, she's not. So I'm going to let her have her moment.

She kisses and sucks her way down my chest. Her thumb brushes my nipple and I jerk. I feel her smile against my abs before she licks the groove of them. Each and every one, she studies carefully, almost as if she's cataloging what makes me groan and pant and jerk.

Then again, she *is* a scientist. It wouldn't surprise me in the slightest if she treats this as another experiment.

She kisses my pelvis, then the line where my thigh meets my groin. She drags her nose along my cock, inhaling deeply.

"Rach…"

Slowly, so fucking slowly, she wraps her hand around my aching shaft and gives me a loose stroke. Her eyes flick up to mine, molten honey.

"Yes?" she asks, like she has no fucking clue how crazy she's driving me. Her tongue darts out to lick her lips. The sensation of her hot breath on the tip of my dick sends a burst of pre-cum from me.

"Please." My voice breaks.

Her grip tightens on me. It's still not enough.

"Please what?" That innocent smile on her lips taunts me. She licks at the dribble of pre-cum rolling down my length with the tip of her tongue, barely touching me.

"Please suck my dick." I gasp out the words. "Please, please, pl—"

Squeezing the base of my cock, she sucks the head of it into her mouth, and my groan rattles through me.

She smirks around me. Her eyes are so fucking expressive. She's enjoying bringing me to my knees.

The hot heat of her mouth engulfs me, her tongue swirling

around the head. Her hand strokes the part of me that won't fit, her grip firm and sure. With her other hand, she reaches between my legs and cups my balls, rolling them in her palm.

My cock jerks in her mouth. Rachel snuffs out a sound that might be amusement before she refocuses her attention on my cock, bobbing her head, sucking on the upstroke.

"Babe…" I'm a prime athlete in peak condition, but the way she makes me feel, I'm breathing hard like I've never run a hundred yards before.

Running a hand through her hair, I hold her close, giving her room to pull back if she needs it. My thumb strokes over her hollowed cheek as she sucks on the tip of my dick.

"You look so fucking pretty, my cock in your mouth," I tell her. "You're doing so good."

She lets out a soft pant, her eyes dark and locked on mine.

"You're taking me so well. It's like you were made to suck my cock." The words pour out of me. "Look at you. Are you wet, baby? Do you like this?"

Rachel lets out a barely audible whine.

"Touch yourself. Touch yourself while you suck my dick."

Her hand dives between her legs. I can barely stand it as she slides two fingers inside her pussy. She pulls them out, then sinks them in again, and when she withdraws a second time, I can see her glistening.

"Change of plans," I announce.

She makes a questioning noise.

Reaching for her, I pull her off my cock and grab her by her shoulders to get her up to my level.

And then I go to work.

Maneuvering her to her back, I dive between her legs, throwing them over each shoulder before I feast myself on her pussy. My fingers slide easily inside her tight, wet heat. She tastes absolutely delicious, salty and musky and so, so perfect. It's like she was made for me, or I was made for her, or both. I could do this for the rest of my life.

And I will. Happily.

My pace is furious, my mouth relentless as I work at her. A fresh burst of wetness erupts on my tongue and I groan at her taste, increasing the force of my fingers inside her.

Rachel's hands slide into my hair, pushing my face closer. Her hips rise, trying to meet me.

With my forearm, I bear down hard on her lower belly above her pelvis, keeping her where I want her.

She comes with a cry, her walls fluttering around my fingers.

Bringing her down slowly, I adjust my pressure and pace without retreating all the way. It's only when she tugs on my hair that I crawl up her body, kissing my way up to her lips.

She's waiting for me, wrapping her arms around me. "That was…"

"Good?"

"More than good." She's breathing hard, too. "Freaking fantastic."

A pleased smile blooms over my face, and as I lean down to kiss her, she runs her hand over my cheek. I nuzzle into the contact instead, seeking her affection. She gives it freely.

There's never any hesitation with her, not when we're like this. It's like as soon as she was over the mental hurdle, she gave herself freely to this. To us.

Rachel inhales deeply, then rolls away. I sling my arm around her waist, holding her close.

"Where're you going?" I murmur. My cock aches, my stomach tight at the thought of her leaving.

"Nightstand."

Releasing her, she crawls across the mattress to the bedside table, pulling out a condom and tossing it to me. As I roll it over my length, she returns to my side and gets on her hands and knees.

I like to see her face when she comes, but I know she also likes when I blanket her body with mine, surrounding her.

She likes to sleep with me half on top of her, too. I don't understand how it can be comfortable, but she's made clear it's her preference, so I'm going to give her what she wants.

That's all I want. For her to have everything she wants.

Notching my cockhead at her entrance, I wait for her to take a deep breath and exhale before I slowly push inside. She's so freaking tight, absolutely perfect, like she was made for me. It's my turn to take a deep breath before I erupt. I want to make this good for her.

Exhaling slowly, I drape myself over her back and wrap my arms around her. She covers my hand with hers, holding me to her.

And then I start to move with short, shallow thrusts. Rachel lets out a soft sigh and lets her head hang low. She arches against me, meeting each thrust.

Each time I pull out and slide back in, my heart gives a loud thump in my chest.

Rachel lets out a low groan, and as her walls start to flutter around me, gripping me so tightly I nearly black out, I let loose my control. It takes another three, four thrusts before I tip over the edge, pleasure barreling into me like a freight train.

I have just enough awareness to collapse beside her on the bed, then pull her down on top of me so I don't crush her.

"Mm." She curls into me.

"Love you," I murmur, before exhaustion hits.

And then I black out.

seventeen

· · ·

Rachel

SNOW FALLS STEADILY OVERNIGHT. When I wake up to an email that school has been canceled due to the storm, I crawl back into bed and steal more of Jake's body heat. He doesn't mind.

We wake up for real a few hours later to the bleating of his alarm. He rolls over to turn it off, then nuzzles into me, still half-asleep. Lying in the comfort of his arms, I card my hand through his short hair.

How did I end up here? How did I go from not even thinking about him to being in a situationship with my ex's younger brother?

Except that's not quite true.

Jake is more than a high school ex's brother. He's a person in his own right, and the truth of the matter is, we probably have more in common than I ever did with Josh. Now that we're adults, the *slight* age difference doesn't bother me—not quite so much as it did a few weeks ago. We never would have worked before now. Good thing it happened when it did.

His hand on my hip grounds me, anchoring me. I'm not

afraid of losing myself in him like I have in past relationships. I know who I am and what I want.

And what I want is Jake.

He releases me and stretches his impressively muscled arms. "I should get up. You have to get to campus."

"Campus is closed for the storm." I burrow into his chest. "I don't have to go in."

He chuckles. "I bet I still have practice."

Grabbing his phone, he flicks through it and makes a surprised noise.

"What?"

"No practice today or tomorrow." He tosses his phone to the side. "We have a game the night after, provided the storm has cleared."

"So… what do we do until then?" I prop myself up on my elbows, blinking innocently at him.

With a laugh, he lunges for me, tackling me back to the bed.

"You're not going anywhere," he teases, before he leans down and kisses me.

I wrap my arms around his shoulders, holding him to me.

"Good. I wasn't planning on it."

As he peppers my neck with kisses, I let myself relax and enjoy the moment.

There's so much to figure out. So much to talk through. For now, I'm just going to enjoy it.

Later, after we're sweaty and sated, we take a shower. He shampoos my hair and massages my back as he washes me, and I take extra care soaping him up and touching every inch of him that I can.

We curl up on his leather sofa in our sweatpants and t-shirts, my head on his chest. I'm a little worried about crushing him, but as he's said repeatedly, he can handle it. I guess there are perks to having a hockey player boyfriend. His being able to throw my weight around is just one of them.

"You know what?" Jake says, his hand on my back.

"Hm?" I look at him.

"The storm means you probably shouldn't drive to New Hampshire."

The thought had occurred to me. "I want to, but it's probably not a great idea."

He clears his throat. "I have three days off next week for the league's Christmas break," he says slowly.

My eyebrows arch up. "You want to celebrate Christmas?"

Jake laughs. "No. But we have the time off, and Chanukah being so late this year that it overlaps…"

I wait.

"Well, why don't we invite your mom to come visit? You can take her to a game," he says.

"You want my mother to come visit?" I repeat.

He nods. "I thought… well, I want to go with you, but I won't have that much time to get away to New Hampshire and back with my playing schedule. And this way you still get to see your mom for the holiday."

There's a lump in my throat, and when I swallow around it, my eyes start to water. The holidays are always hard since losing my dad four years ago.

"Oh. Shit. No. Don't cry." His thumb brushes beneath my eye. "Only if you're ready for it."

"I want you to meet my mom," I tell him. "Properly, that is."

He heaves out a sigh of relief. "Good. Because I want that, too."

I swallow. "Maybe…"

Jake waits patiently for me to get my thought out.

"Maybe your parents can come, too," I blurt.

He beams at me. "You want to meet my parents?"

"Yeah. I think—I think I should."

Threading his hand through my hair, he brings me close for a sweet kiss. "That sounds great."

I clear my throat. "I also—I think we should talk to Josh first."

"He's going to be pissed," Jake says.

"I know."

"He pretty much hates me," he continues.

"He's your brother. He doesn't—"

He shakes his head. "We don't get along. He's going to insinuate that this is me trying to get back at him for some perceived slight."

"It's not, though." I know it in my bones. He cares about me. This isn't a game.

With some of my exes, yeah, I might have second guessed things.

With him? I know where we stand.

"It's not," Jake agrees. "My feelings for you are entirely separate from him. But given how much of a dick he is on a normal day…"

"We can't be afraid of him," I tell him. "It doesn't have to go over well. It probably won't. He still deserves to know."

He sighs. "We'll tell him."

I grab my phone, opening up my contacts.

"Wait, now?" he asks, staring at my phone like it's a poisonous spider.

"Let's get it over with."

But as I scroll through my contacts, I don't find Josh Lewis in there. I've had the same phone number since I was thirteen, all of my contacts are backed up to the cloud… and he's not there.

"Huh."

"What?" Jake presses a kiss to my temple.

"I must have deleted him from my phonebook."

He chuckles. "Is that because he's a worthless dickbag?"

Or maybe I just don't care about him anymore.

Elbowing him, I reach for Jake's phone, holding it up to

his face to unlock the screen. He chuckles as I scroll through his phonebook.

There are three other Joshes in his address book, all with last names, and then there's an all-lowercase **josh** entry. I click on it and, sure enough, it's our old area code.

I click on a video call and the line rings. Once, twice, three times. Finally, on the fourth ring, it connects.

Josh's face comes into view from below. He's gotten older. Then again, we both have. He has a beard now and lines on his face.

"What do you want, asshole?" Josh snaps.

Jake takes the phone from me. "I wanted to talk to you."

"Bullshit," Josh says. "Pull the other one."

"I did. I wanted to ask you a question."

He rolls his eyes. "So ask it, already. I have to get back to work."

Jake blows out a breath, and Josh pauses, looking up at the screen and doing a double-take.

"Wait. Are you with a chick? Why are you calling me?"

Pulling on Jake's arm, I tilt the camera until I'm in view, too.

"Hi, Josh."

My high school boyfriend blinks a few times. "Rachel? Rachel Levine?"

I let out a nervous giggle. "Hi."

Jake tightens his arm around me and brushes a kiss to my temple.

"What are you doing with *him*?" His disbelief is clear to see.

"We're together," I tell him.

"I can see that," Josh says evenly. "Why?"

"Because I love her," Jake returns.

My stomach swoops, and I look up at him. He's smiling down at me, his eyes bright.

"I love you," he repeats.

"I love you, too," I tell him.

He beams at me.

A gag makes me remember the video call.

"Gross," Josh says.

"We wanted you to be the first to know," Jake says. "I know you guys have history, but—"

To my surprise, his brother laughs. "Dude, that was, like, fifteen years ago. That's in the past."

I swallow. "So you're not upset?"

Josh shakes his head. "Seriously, Rach. You were great, but we were never going to work. We were kids. I'm happy you've found someone who makes you happy." He pauses. "Even if he is a supreme dick."

Jake flips him off.

Shaking my head, I let out a nervous laugh. "We're inviting the parents up for Chanukah. Do... do you want to come?"

Josh pauses. "Yeah, I guess so," he finally says. His lip curls. "It'll be... fun."

"It will be," Jake says firmly. "If you wanted to bring your girlfriend..."

"We broke up," Josh says shortly.

"Oh. I'm sorry."

"Yeah, well." He shrugs. "I'll come visit. Maybe Rach can set me up with one of her friends."

I laugh. "Sure, bud."

There's a clang behind him. "Shit. Gotta go." He pauses again. "I'm happy for you two. Really."

And then the call disconnects.

I look up at Jake. "That went... better than expected."

"I'm pleasantly surprised," he agrees. He leans down and kisses me. "Now let's hope the rest of our family is as supportive."

"They will be."

Jake smirks at me. "Oh? And how do you know?"
"Because they want us to be happy."
He pinches my side. "And are you happy?"
Nodding, I nuzzle his neck. "Very."
Jake tips my chin up, pressing the softest kiss to my lips.
"Good. Because you make me happy, too."

epilogue

. . .

Jake

THE DOORBELL RINGS, and Rachel wrings her hands.

"Breathe," I tell her, squeezing her shoulder, as I scoot past her to the door.

On the front stoop are my parents. Behind them is my brother Jeremy, a mile-wide grin on his face.

"Jakey!" My mom pulls me into a hug.

"Hi, Ma. How was the drive?" I pat her back gently.

Dad prods her inside the apartment, giving me a firm handshake. Jer pauses to clap me on the back.

As I close the door, I'm surprised when my brother crosses the room to Rachel and lifts her clear off her feet in a hug.

She giggles, hugging him back. "Hey, Jer."

"I'm so glad this happened," Jeremy says. He winks outrageously. "You know the third time's the charm, right? I'm the third brother."

Rachel laughs. "I think I'm good with Jake, thanks."

Ma raises her brows. "So you're together?"

When I nod, my mom lets out a squeal.

"Oh, I knew it!" She kisses me loudly on the cheek and squeezes me about the middle. Towering over her like I have since the week before my bar mitzvah, she only comes halfway up my torso. "I'm so happy for you two!"

"Thanks, Ma." I pat her on the back again until she releases me.

We move farther into the apartment, which Rachel has decorated perfectly. The black, white, and chrome has been softened by the blue and white garland above the mantle and matching tablecloth over the dining room table she had brought in. The little gnomes sit on the coffee table, staring serenely out at us.

"I haven't been here in forever," Dad says as he looks around the living room. "I like what you've done with the place."

"Oh, it's all Rachel," I deflect.

I didn't exactly decorate after I bought the place. Jeremy didn't care what was on the walls or if there were knickknacks on the console table. In the last few weeks, Rachel's made the place her own—or rather, *ours*. She's asked me before acquiring each new thing, even though I've told her she has free rein. Her favorite thing to do when we're unwinding on the couch is to look through interior decorating websites and point things out to me.

And whatever makes her smile and brings her joy, I buy. Because I want her to be happy. I like when she smiles. I like bringing her joy.

The doorbell rings again, and I excuse myself to open the door.

Mrs. Levine stands on the doorstep, holding a casserole dish.

"Hello, Mrs. Levine," I greet, ushering her in. "Let me get that for you."

"Oh, you sweet boy," she says, pushing it into my hands. "I made a kugel."

My stomach rumbles. "Potato or noodle?"

"Noodle. With enough cheese to clog your arteries," she says cheerfully.

"I can't wait." My smile is genuine as I deposit it in the kitchen and peer under the foil. It smells delicious. The scent of sweet cheese and noodles makes my mouth water. It is definitely not part of the diet plan. Luckily, it's a holiday, and I don't play until tomorrow night.

Ma catches me peeking under the foil and shakes her head. "You're hungry?"

"I'm always hungry," I defend.

Rachel has been cooking for the last two days while I've been on a road trip to Pittsburgh. She made a delicious sweet and sour brisket plus a vat of matzo ball soup, stuffed cabbage, and roasted sweet potatoes to go with the potato latkes I fried this morning and have warming in the oven. To cut some of the heaviness of the holiday food, I also made a green salad and roasted asparagus.

My parents brought a challah, my favorite chocolate and cherry rugelach, and sufganiyot, the traditional jelly donuts we eat on Chanukah.

"Is it time yet?" Jer asks, peeking into the kitchen.

"Just waiting on one more," Rachel says, giving me a happy smile from across the room.

And sure enough, when the bell rings a few minutes later, she looks calm and relaxed. She joins me at the door.

Josh looks good. He's trimmed his beard, though his hair is as long as ever, and he's wearing a clean button-up shirt and nice jeans. He blinks at the sight of us and then breaks into a huge grin.

"Hey, Josh," Rachel says with a smile. "It's good to see you."

"You, too," he says, and I believe him to be genuine.

Stepping back, I let him enter the house, and he gives her a tight hug, whispering something into her ear. She smiles and giggles, then releases him.

My oldest brother claps me on the back. "You did good with this one, kid."

"Thanks," I mutter, because even though I don't want his approval, it does feel nice to receive it.

"Don't fuck it up," he mutters under his breath before he pushes past me. "Hey, Ma."

Josh ducks to let our mother dote on him a bit. She smooths his messy curls. He lives in New Hampshire, same as they do, but on the opposite side of the city. I don't think he goes home much.

I can't blame him. I love my parents. I love them more from a distance.

"Let's light the candles," Rachel says.

The menorah is already set up on the kitchen island, with five candles placed for the fifth night of Chanukah. Each night so far, we've lit the candles together, and when I was on the road for our two-night trip, we did it together over video chat.

I hand Rachel the matches and she lights the candles, and then together, we say the blessings as a group. After, we sit for dinner, my dad at one end of the table and myself at the other. Rachel sits beside me, passing me the challah and then the wine to say the blessings. The familiar Hebrew words are comforting. I've known these prayers since I was in preschool. They're an intrinsic part of me, of where I've been and where I'm going.

Conversation flows easily as we eat. My mom and Mrs. Levine get along like a house on fire, and before the end of the meal, my mom's invited her to her weekly mahjong game and Mrs. Lewis has promised to share her noodle kugel recipe.

As I expected, it's delicious. She uses crushed pineapple, apricot jelly, and dried cranberries in the sweet, cheesy noodle dish. It shouldn't work together, but it's delicious. It's like a warm hug in casserole form.

Rachel is chatting with Jeremy and my dad, holding her

own. Watching her settle in with my family brings a smile to my face.

And, to my surprise, to Josh's, too.

"You're good?" I mutter to my brother.

He nods. "I'm good. I'm happy for her. For you." He coughs. "It was a little weird at first, but I got used to it. I think you're good for her. And she's definitely good for you."

"She is," I agree, watching as she gesticulates wildly to make her point.

I thought I was happy before, but now I know I was living a half-life. There was never a chance to let myself relax and just be myself. I was too caught up in my career to let anyone in.

And now that I have?

Coming home to Rachel is the highlight of my day. I don't care if she's already asleep. Curling up beside her makes me happy. Cuddled on the couch, grabbing lunch on campus, or going to the bar after my game, all I want is to spend time with her.

I thought I was happy. I thought I was okay. I had no idea what I was missing out on.

Now that I've found her, I'm not going to let her go. With her, wherever she is, I'm home.

———

Want more of Jake and Rachel? Check out their bonus epilogue.

The story continues with Body Check, where recently divorced captain Jason McKittrick finds his happily ever after.

afterword

Thank you for reading *Home for the Holidays*. This book is my baby and I absolutely love it to pieces.

Reviews are more important than readers realize. If you liked this book, please leave me a review!

Join my newsletter to stay in the loop! Lots of unfunny quips, unsuccessful attempts at wit, and general grouching about the writing process.

xoxo,

Allie

what's next?

The story continues with *Defenseless*, where Ryan Logan has been pining for his best friend's little sister since high school. When their 10-year reunion comes around, he makes sure they get to relive the prom night they never got.

Want more of the Neurospicy Book Club? Check out *Sportsball is for Lovers*, featuring Sadie and the super hot guy she meets on a kink app... where she learns that six degrees of separation don't always involve Kevin Bacon...

about the author

Allie is a queer and AuDHD writer with a hyper-fixation on inclusivity and representation. She loves the color purple, Michigan football, the Detroit Lions, and the Boston Bruins. When she's not absorbed by a book, she likes to spend time with her nephews.

A San Diego, CA native now residing in South Carolina, she is allergic to the cold, rain, snow, and mosquitos.

also by allie lasky

Meet the Neurospicy Book Club in The Thought of You, where grumpy Johanna finds out she's autistic… because her happy-go-lucky new roomie (and reformed playboy ex-football player) has to tell her.

———

For more Own Voices, try Spark: A Chanukah Novella, where neurodivergent Arielle and her childhood friend Asher finally connect after two decades of missed chances.

———

Want to see how it all started? Read <u>The Game Plan</u> to meet sweet cinnamon roll football player Miles and the feisty sorority girl who stole his heart.

www.ingramcontent.com/pod-product-compliance
Lightning Source LLC
Chambersburg PA
CBHW061354310726
48974CB00001B/338